THE CADILLAC KIND

THE CADILLAC KIND

MAUREEN FOSS

POLESTAR
BOOK PUBLISHERS

The Cadillac Kind
Copyright © 1996 by Maureen Foss

The publisher would like to thank the Canada Council, the British Columbia Ministry of Small Business, Tourism and Culture, and the Department of Canadian Heritage for their ongoing financial assistance.

Cover photograph by Henry Kalen
Cover design by Jim Brennan
Editing by Betsy Nuse
Printed and bound in Canada

POLESTAR BOOK PUBLISHERS
1011 Commercial Drive, Second Floor
Vancouver, BC
Canada   V5L 3X1
(604) 251-9718

CANADIAN CATALOGUING IN PUBLICATION DATA
Foss, Maureen.
  The Cadillac kind
ISBN 1-896095-10-0
    I. Title.
PS8561.07725C32 1996   C813'.54   C96-910010-8
PR9199.3F571C32 1996

To my writing companions
Rosella, Gwen, Eileen and Betty

I knew when I drained the third glass that I shouldn't have, but by then it was too late. I had skunked Bernie at crib and was feeling just a tad superior, when the bugger leaned back on the hind legs of his chair, reached those long fingers around the bottle of wine, tipped forward, then poured. The label said Baby Duck but I knew it was Bernie's Best Blackberry. The whole thing was a set-up, the skunk crib game and all. Before I knew it, I had agreed with Verna that it really would be fun to take our mother to Manitoba to visit her sister. And I would drive from Vancouver. I don't remember that part, but both Verna and Bernard said it truly happened. They swore on the soul of their Volkswagen beetle. That was the other reason I had volunteered to drive, they said: I had a '65 Mercedes with a split front seat that reclined, more comfortable for Mother.

"THAT'S THE FIRST BAG I PUT IN THE TRUNK, Mother. Why would you put your glasses in the very first bag? I am not going to rummage around now."

We haven't gone three blocks. I'm sure I still see Verna and the kids waving in the rear-view mirror, laughing fit to kill.

"Do you have any spares you can wear until we stop for lunch?" She's sucking her tooth. The gold one, third from the front, left side. The side closest to me. "You mad at me already?"

"No," says Mother tightly, looking straight ahead, clutching her newest Danielle Steele novel.

"Alright. I'll get the bloody glasses."

"No need to be testy, Edith. It's not called for."

"You're one to talk."

A light drizzle soaks through my shirt as I replace Mother's bags and her laundry basket of dried flower heads, her potpourri.

I hand her the glasses. "Thank you. You're most kind," Mother says, face composed, lips unmoving.

She should be a ventriloquist. Maybe ... maybe she's the

one who suggested the drive to Manitoba and Verna thought it was me. She threw her voice, and Verna naturally figured … I look over but the eyes behind the glasses are closed.

"I thought you wanted to read?"

"No need to be touchy. I'll get around to it."

It's going to be a long trip.

"Then why don't you tilt the seat back and have a little snooze?" I offer, changing tack. "Your pillow is in the back seat next to the kindling." Mother's taking kindling because she knows they don't have any in Manitoba. It was on sale at K Mart.

"I'm fine, Edith. Just watch the road. You know how you are when it's raining and there are cars all around."

"No, Mother, how am I?" My neck starts to tighten.

"You're using that voice with me, Edith. You think they're all out to get you. It's just a touch of paranoia. Your father had the same thing when he was institutionalized." She folds her glasses, puts them into her purse, then pulls the lever next to the seat. The back falls from behind her with such force that in the tumble her patent leather shoes slam the underside of the dashboard. Sounds like two rifle shots. The kicks knock CBC radio right off the air. Her paisley print skirt slides up her legs, pleating itself against the seatbelt. She grabs the air trying to right herself.

"What is that?" I ask, not really believing what I'm seeing.

"It's me falling into the back seat," she shrieks. "I'll never walk again."

"No, no, what's that on your leg?"

"Just drive, Edith, and mind your Ps and Qs." She tugs the skirt down over her knees.

"You're wearing a garter, for chrissake."

"It's not for Christ's sake, it's for mine. It's to hold up my stockings," says Mother, bringing the seat upright in stages.

"Red lace to hold up pantyhose?" I laugh. She turns her back to me. "Mother?" It appears that for the next sixty miles I'll have the dismal weather and myself for company.

I sing Willie Nelson's "On the Road Again" because that's what he would sing if he had to drive his mother to Manitoba.

▲

"I have to get gas in Hope, Mum. Would you like something to eat?" It wasn't thunder rumbling in the distance. Mother's stomach will not be silent until fed. "Come on, I'll buy you a cup of coffee." My power of persuasion carries more weight when food is mentioned.

I drive the car to the back of the Chicken Coop Café and stop with the nose pointing downhill. The starter has been acting up so I park on grades. I remove the rock from behind the driver's seat and kick it under the rear wheel. The emergency brake has a mind of its own.

Mother and I slide into a red vinyl booth facing the highway. Blurred faces peer through wet windows in cars passing by. Drops of water shimmer on mother's hair like a coronet on a mauve cloud.

"Your hair looks nice, Mum."

"Why, thank you, Edith," she says, relaxing against the back of the seat. "Bruce at the Klip and Kurl calls this colour Sexy Senior. He's such a dear. He's trying to line me up with his father." She rummages through her purse, finding the tiny mirror attached to her lipstick case. Waving it before her face, she checks for personal defects. Finding none, she puts the mirror away.

"Did you meet him?"

"Who?"

"Bruce's father."

"Oh, he cruised the shop as Bruce was applying my hair colour. There I sat," she illustrates, "with a plastic halo thing around my head, looking like a satellite dish. I refused Bruce's offer of an introduction. Old dad looked interesting though, in a hairy-chested sort of way. Just the opposite of Bruce." She polishes the top of the napkin dispenser and rearranges the salt and pepper to stand guard on either side of it.

"Nice to see cheerful travellers. Can I get you ladies anything?" the waitress inquires, pad in hand.

I ask for coffee. Mother gazes longingly toward the pies displayed in their tiered glass condominiums.

"I think I'll have ... no, no, I shouldn't."

"Eat a little something, Mum," I encourage. "It'll be a long day."

"OK, I'll try. I'll have ... do you make your own pies?"

The waitress sighs, and shifts her weight to the other foot. "Me, personally? No, ma'am. We have pie gnomes chained in the kitchen."

"Well," Mother huffs, feathers ruffled. "I was only asking."

"I'm sorry," says the waitress, whose nametag reads PEG. "I've got a headache. Must be a full moon."

Mother softens. "Would you like an aspirin, dear? Edith, move over and let her sit down. She has a headache."

Peg flips her order book into her frilly brown apron. "How 'bout I bring you ladies your order then I'll join you. You like apple? Little ice cream on top? Gotcha."

"Mother!" I sigh, as Peg departs.

"Oh, Edith. Put a cork in it." Mum busies herself wiping the table, just in case Peg missed anything.

Only fifteen hundred miles to go, more or less.

"Do you have to go to the bathroom before we leave, Edith?"

"I'm forty-two, y'know. I make those decisions myself now." I pay the bill.

"You remember how you are, Edith. Soon's we get underway, you'll have to pee."

"Mother, will you lower your voice? People are looking."

She takes offense. "Nobody cares about your bladder,

Edith. Not even me." Her heel squeals as she does an about-face. She mutters her way down the orange-stuccoed corridor, past the door marked ROOSTERS, to the HENS entrance. It clucks as it closes behind her.

Walking to the car alone, I whistle "Ain't Nobody Here But Us Chickens" with just the traffic noise and the hiss of rain as backup.

While waiting for Mother to reappear I decide it's a good time to reconnect the radio to whatever wires look orphaned. In order to see, I drape my legs over the seat back, feet dangling above the kindling, head hanging under the dash. There are grey wires, red, blue. Plastic bits connecting wire to wire. I figure red goes with red, blue with blue. Pretty simple, really, and I don't even need a chainsaw.

I'm still under there when a damp breeze and the interior light floods the floor area. "We shall have music wherever we go. Bodee oh doh," I croon for Mother's benefit.

From the open door I hear a gold tooth being sucked. "Charleen, the shadetree mechanic down there is my daughter, Edith. She's the driver."

My collar catches on the gas pedal as my legs bicycle the air. Peering from under the dash, I see Mother and a head of hair in black leotards. The hair is doing its best to grow over the face beneath it. I grunt my way upright and shift behind the wheel before nodding in the stranger's direction. Mother climbs in first, brushing the rain from her clothes. The hair slides in beside her, slams the door then lifts her packsack over her head and discards it behind the seat right onto my glass jars. Mother brings sticks of cedar kindling to Manitoba; I bring brandied peaches, pickled walnuts and geranium jelly. Things too good to let the birds eat.

"Charleen? Is that what Mother called you?"

She nods.

"Can I help you, Charleen?" I hone the edge on my voice, sharpening my tongue.

"Yeah, the ride'll do real nice," says Charleen.

"You'll notice this is a two-seater, and the back seat's full."

"We'll share this one," Mum says, squeezing closer to me.

"I don't mind." She waves her fingers in the direction of the ignition. "Drive!"

The car starts first try. The emergency brake even disengages. First gear drops in with barely a grind. I release the clutch but the car doesn't move. Again the clutch is depressed and released. Nothing. The engine dies.

"The rock, Edith," Mother hisses, jabbing with her elbow. "You forgot the rock."

I hate it when she's right. I pull the emergency brake on before opening the door to retrieve the rock and replace it behind the seat. Charleen hunches over the unlit dial on the radio.

"So," I manage, "you need a ride, eh?" I check left before entering the highway. By the time I've shifted into high gear she still hasn't answered. "You need a ride? To where, exactly?" *Please let it be the bus depot, three blocks away.*

"Bangkok."

"Thailand? Bangkok, Thailand?" I ask, showing all those years of Social Studies are not wasted.

"Chill out. It's a joke, right." The girl and my mother laugh. My mother, who doesn't even get knock-knock jokes.

I exhale twice ... heh ... heh. "No, really, seriously, where are you going?" I whine.

"Think I'll try Banff. Gonna get work there." She pushes both hands into her hair and scrubs vigorously. "Gawd, that feels good. Haven't had a bath for a week or two," she reveals, examining the contents of her fingernails.

"Charleen said she's been sleeping in a tree house," volunteers Mother. "Poor thing. I told her we'd be happy to give her a ride." Mother reaches to pat Charleen's knee lumping beneath the seasoned leotards, but instead vacillates over the area like a healer looking for disease. She brings her hand back and crosses her arms, wiping the palm down her sleeve, just in case. "She was drying her underwear with that hot air machine in the bathroom at the restaurant. Isn't that clever?"

"Never got them dry enough. They're sticking to my bum." Mother laughs, then realizes it isn't offered as humour.

"I'll probably get a cold from all this rain. Plus the wet underwear." Charleen squirms just thinking about it. "Gawd, I get so much phlegm when I get a cold." She tries a tentative cough but gets no satisfactory expectoration. "I'm beat. D'ya mind if I pass out for awhile? Got a pillow?"

"No," says Mother quickly.

"Sure, Charleen. Mum's pillow is in the back seat. Just help yourself." Through my clothes I feel Mother reaching for a sizeable piece of skin she can pinch.

⟁

"The engine's running a little warm, Mum. I'll stop at Yale to check the water and oil. Can't be too careful. Wouldn't want anything to happen on our trip, no siree."

"So, we're looking for a garage with a bathroom, are we, Edith?" she gloats. "What did I tell you?"

I hate it when she's right. I hate it!

For the sake of appearances, I ask the attendant to check the oil while I sneak off to the Ladies. Gasoline rainbows arc across the wet blacktop.

When I return to the Mercedes, its front door is agape and Charleen's spindle-shanks sprawl through the opening. "Whatcha doing?" I ask.

"Fixing this goddam radio. The fucker won't work."

Mum sits bolt upright. Her eyes, usually dime size, are as big as silver dollars. She gnaws her thumbnail as Charleen works at her feet.

"I wouldn't worry about it," I tell her. "Can't get much going through the canyon anyway."

"I've almost got the mother rewired." She thrusts both hands under the dash like a midwife at a birthing. "There, done. Some idiot hooked the wires up ass-backwards."

The dial's now lit and the speakers hum. Charleen jostles Mum aside to make room for herself, then slams the door, saying, "Let's roll." She licks her fingers before twisting the knobs, like in the movies when the thief has his ear to the door of the safe and he's about to figure out the combination.

"Hey, Edith, why you driving a beater like this? You on welfare or something? This radio's shitty." Charleen boots it with the crusty toe of her leotard. Her unoccupied sandals are hardening beneath the air vent.

"The radio works but it only gets CBC. It's all I ever listen to anyway," I explain, although I wonder why I bother.

"CBC is crap," Charleen offers. "They're always telling you stuff. Playing artsy-fartsy music alla time. No U2. No Stones. Where's Kool Moe Dee? I bet you old ladies never even heard of Rap. Ever see Skinny Puppy? Beastie Boys? You guys have 8-track at home with Barry Manilow and Nat King Cole, or what?"

"What do you mean old ladies?" Mother is using her High Noon, reach-for-your-gun-pardner voice. Smooth, slow, well-enunciated. Still makes the hair rise on the back of my neck. That tone has stopped my sister Verna and me dead in our tracks. Used to freeze my father like a pointer spotting game.

We pass a road sign warning Spuzzum ahead. Mother reaches behind the seat, hooks the backpack on her fingers. "Charleen wants off in Spuzzum," she announces. "Charleen is going to find a ride with a trucker. A trucker with a radio. And a pillow. Edith, pull in behind that rig," she dictates. "Get your sandals on, Toots, you're outta here."

Charleen glares ahead and hugs the backpack to her congested chest. When we stop, she opens the door and steps outside, flailing her arms through the straps to shift the canvas load onto her back.

"Thanks for nothing, you old bitch," Charleen says, slamming the door.

Mother rolls the window down halfway and thrusts her face into the gap, "I hope he has a social disease." She cranks up the glass.

Charleen crosses the lot, giving us a stiffly raised middle

finger. She dodges puddles as she heads towards the parked transport truck.

Mother rolls the window down again and hisses, "Little fucker." The retaliation was carried away on the wind.

I look askance at my scented, lilac-haired Mother. The president of the bridge club, treasurer of the African Violet Club (Variegated Leaf Division).

Our departure scatters gravel over the Spuzzum parking lot.

Being a wet laugher, I must pull over a quarter mile away to wipe away the tears. Mum guffaws now and again on the way to Kamloops.

I know Mrs. Nelson wouldn't use language like that. She'd probably hum while crocheting covers for the head-rests on Willie's truck.

"What do you mean we're not going to make Calgary? I'm perfectly fine now. It was just a little indigestion," she says, suppressing a burp. "We made good time to Kamloops and I'm not tired a bit. We'll make Calgary, Edith, no problem." Mother reapplies lipstick onto her moving mouth. No problem comes out as "gno pom pom."

"It may be 'gno pom pom' for you but it's a big 'pom pom' for me."

"Edith, what are you talking about?"

"I'm not driving all the way to Calgary in one day."

"You neglected to tell me this, Edith. This I did not know! Do you realize Aunt Ida and Aunt Rhetta are expecting us?"

"You neglected to tell me this, Mother," I echo. "Maybe if you hadn't ordered roast suckling pig for lunch we might have made it. How can Aunt Ida and Aunt Rhetta be expecting us unless you took it upon yourself to tell them to expect us?"

"Well, they're sort of expecting us."

"What kind of 'sort'?" I ask suspiciously.

"I said we'd be passing through and they said, 'give us a call'." She folds her arms decisively.

"That's it?" I say, gearing down as we labour behind a motorhome. "They just said, give us a call?"

"Yes, Edith, 'give us a call'."

"That's hardly 'expecting us'. It's more like, 'if you're near a phone and have two bits to spare, drop it in. If we're home we may answer'." An impatient string of cars bunches up behind us.

"Bloody motorhomes should be outlawed. Move over you jerk." I gear down again, trapped in its blue exhaust, angry at the rear bumper sticker forewarning, IF THIS MOTOR-HOME'S A-ROCKIN' — DON'T COME KNOCKIN'.

"So," says Mother, nipping at the tail end of the argument, "as driver and supreme being in this automobile, where have you decided we should stay?" She waves her hanky under her nose. "Pass him," she directs.

The driver slows to check a roadside map and I use the opportunity, swerving the car outward to peer past the motorhome. An approaching van bears down upon us, blatting its horn before fading into the distance. I try again and see a break in the traffic ahead. I pull alongside the tortoise-like shell of the motorhome. The driver, a moon-faced man chewing a stubby cigar, sits on his lofty padded perch above the throng.

"You asshole," I shout, leaning past Mother to shake my fist. He smiles and waves as we surge past. I step on the gas, happy to be ahead. CBC is fading in and out. I have a warning throb in my temple.

"Edith?"

I grunt a reply.

"When a police car has its lights blinking, doesn't that mean stop, or something?"

I check the rear-view mirror and see red and blue flashes,

much like those signaling a migraine. "Oh my god. Oh my god."

"Pull over. It's probably nothing. I'll drive if they jail you." She sounds delighted.

"Ohmygodohmygod. My license? Where is it? Where's my purse? The registration?" I see the officer allowing the motorhome to proceed before he exits his car. The man in the motorhome leans forward to wave the cigar as he passes.

"Afternoon, ladies," says the highway patrolman, but his greeting doesn't come across as truly sincere.

"Good afternoon, officer," chirps my mother. "Lovely now that we've outrun the rain."

"Wha? Wha?" My mouth is dry. I try swallowing but make a sound like toenails on a bathroom floor. Policemen have this effect on me.

"May I see your driver's license, please, ma'am?" He slides his hat back off his forehead and I look into the mirrored sunglasses, seeing myself guppy-like. "Your license, please."

Mother jabs me into action. I spill the contents of my handbag into my lap and rummage through the papers, keys, elastics ...

"You women sure hold a lot of junk in a small space," observes the policeman.

Bugger off, you big stupid flatfoot. "Silly me, here it is," I fawn.

"Take it out of the wallet, please."

I hand it over with my thumb covering the photo. I hate that picture. I was dislodging a sesame seed from my tooth when they took the damn thing. Looks like I was in mid-seizure.

He looks from the picture to me and back again. His eyebrows rise above the mirrored lenses. I force a smile. "Terrible, isn't it?"

"Looks just like you," he says dryly, returning the card. *Smartass.* "Where are you ladies heading in such a hurry?"

"Manitoba," says Mum. "Going to visit my sister Queenie. My OLDER sister. Her birthday is the eleventh of September, and we're going there for a little celebration."

"Stationed there in my early days. Couldn't get out fast enough." He turns his attention to me. "What's your occupation, Miss?"

"Writer," I say, refilling my purse.

"Ha!"

He leans in the window, peering at my passenger. "Did you say 'Ha!', ma'am?"

"Ha!" repeats my mother.

"Are you a writer or not?" He scowls as he re-checks his notebook where my name is written. "Miss, uh, Flood."

"I get paid for writing which makes me a writer."

"Have I read any of your stuff?" He curls his lip. "Or do you write romances?"

"You have probably read quite a bit of my *stuff*, as you call it. Everybody does at some time or other."

"Edith Flood? Edith Flood? Nope, just doesn't ring a bell. So, what do you write?"

"Sears catalogue."

"Come again," he says. Mother sniffs into her hanky.

"I write the text in the Sears catalogue. You know, 'a gift to treasure! This ultra-feminine stocking and garter set comes in three thrilling colours. Beige, off-white and sand.' That kind of stuff."

"Hey, I didn't know a real person wrote that. I dunno, I guess I thought it just sort of rolled out of a computer." He folds his black book into his pocket. "Interesting. Well, you ladies have a good trip and drive carefully."

My heartbeat is slowing somewhat. Jail is not around the corner. Mother will be disappointed. "S'cuse me," I call to his retreating back. "What did you stop me for?"

He slaps his forehead with an open palm and returns. "Meeting a real writer threw me, you know?"

Oh puleeze. "You passed that motorhome without signalling. The vehicle following cannot read your mind. You gotta give him some kind of hint, you know? A little clue." His thumbnail makes a rasping sound as he scratches his chin. "That's it, lecture over. You can go." He nods once then strides to his car.

"Some cop," Mother comments. "Didn't even check the registration. I wanna be frisked for concealed weapons. Maybe we're car thieves driving to our 'chop house'. It's my duty to call him back."

"Mother, you open your mouth again and you're walking."

"It was a joke, Edith. Chill, dude."

Shades of Charleen. "You're incorrigible. By the way, Mother, a 'chop house' is a restaurant. Stolen cars are dismantled at a 'chop shop'. I saw it on '60 Minutes', too."

"Whatever." She removes her shoes and wiggles her toes under the fresh air vent. "Let's go. If my feet heat up then my ankles swell."

With the rain left behind at Spuzzum, the sun warms the late summer day. We continue east toward our Manitoba Mecca.

"You want to look around Banff before we find a place to stay, Mum?" She had fallen asleep with her hand folded under her face. As she straightens in her seat, I see the rosy imprint of four fingers tattooed on her cheek. "You want to check out a few stores before we get a room?"

Mother is slow to reply as she squints at the sidewalks busy with people. A car pulls out before me so I park while awaiting her answer, which doesn't come. "I need to stretch my legs," I say, coaxing her. "Let's take a break."

After she combs her hair and repairs her makeup, we lean into the late afternoon heat. A tourist town, alright. Japanese visitors with their high-tech equipment photograph each other near totem poles and gift shops. Craggy stone mountains provide the soft focus background.

Mother and I enter the coolness of an ice cream parlour

and we linger before the glass case with the others, deciding from among the tubs of artificially coloured confections. The girl behind the counter sighs as we shuffle the length a second time. Important decision-making can't be rushed. I point out my choice. The girl drops the bottom scoop of chocolate, chocolate-chip into a pink sugar cone, then molds a melting glob of pralines and cream onto the chocolate chocolate-chip. Dark rivulets of melting ice cream roll down the cone into the surrounding paper. Mother chooses a double pumpkin and licorice without much hemming and hawing.

"That's quite a combination, Mum. Hope you can sleep tonight." We carry our guilty pleasures to a clean table where we can watch the street.

"I picked it so you wouldn't ask for a taste. You always want share-sies."

"Do not," I argue, pulling out a wrought-iron chair.

There's an art to eating ice cream. You have to twirl the cone while your tongue smoothes the edges, blending the two scoops into one neat pyramid of perfection. By the time you tidy the top and make a tip that folds over, the bottom is dripping onto your hand and you start again. But Mother is a biter. Bite, suck, swallow, bite, chew, swallow. When the ice- cream headache hits, she closes her eyes, face screwing up, waiting for the moment of pain to subside before taking the next bite.

Even in here, my shirt sticks to my back. Mum and I fan our faces with the menus while we crunch the last of the cones. Then a shadow blocks the glare from the lowering sun. Outside the window, a faceless body is illuminated from behind. It holds one hand against the glass to look in. The other is upraised, holding the stump of a cigar. The sunset radiates through out-turned ears creating the impression of a dark urn with glowing handles. It waves its fingers at us then leaves the window to enter the door.

"Hello there, ladies. Have a little run-in with the law?" There's an odious smell of cigar. I look up, then drop my sights to where a short rotund form raises and lowers himself on tip toes. His magnified eyes blink behind rounded lenses. "I'm the guy in the motorhome." He bends over me, bobbing. "Remember?" He thrusts his middle finger upward, repeating my highway gesture. "The asshole."

I try to hide my head in my purse.

"Well, hello there. Nice to see you again." The voice sounds familiar. "Won't you join us?" It is familiar. "We're just finishing off our ice cream," says Mother. "So warm out there, isn't it?" She sounds all soft, like a Tennessee Williams' character. *So waaam*.

I give her my look. She won't acknowledge so I kick out, missing her but striking the table leg which shivers the plastic flowers in the vase.

"Suppose the little lady will mind?" he asks.

"Who, Edith? No, no, she doesn't mind in the teeniest." Mother indicates a chair, which he fills with his ample bottom.

I excuse myself. Even after splashing water on my face it burns. Never fails; I show a bit of assertiveness by fingering someone and I get caught. I mean, what are the chances? I'll wait five more minutes. Maybe he'll leave.

"Ready to go, Mother?" I ask when I return. I put a potted plant between her firmly entrenched guest and me.

"Oh, Edith, Walter and I are having such a nice chat."

Walter? "Mu-uth-h-h-er. We have to go," I insist.

"Walter, please excuse me for just a minute." Mother smiles graciously while leaving the table, but that pretense pales as she swoops at me. "Will you wipe that look off your face. I'm having a nice time."

"Well, I'm not sitting in here any longer," I reply stubbornly.

"Good," she says, "get lost for awhile."

"I'll give you a half hour with that ... that ..."

"Gentleman?" says Mother, arching her eyebrows.

"You be ready when I get back or I'll leave you here. I really will." I push the door against the thick afternoon, joining the parade of pedestrians.

She's leaning against the side of the car when I return, laughing with that little man. When he sees me bearing down, he chucks Mother ... MY Mother ... under the chin and saunters away, white suit barely restraining his abundance.

"He looks like a pimple on a hog's ass," I contend, wanting to speed his retreat with a dusty footprint.

"Edith!" she fumes, flinging herself into the car, "That's no way for a lady to talk." She slams the door. "Walter is a charming man."

"You," I say, my volume rising, "just got picked up by a stranger. What if he's an axe murderer?"

She sucks in her cheeks. "I don't think that was an axe he had in his pants, Edith, but you could be right."

I'm sure she muttered "woodsman, prune my tree," but when I ask her to repeat it, she shrugs and smirks. I definitely see a smirk.

"Let's get ourselves a room," she says changing the subject. "With air conditioning and a pool full of gin and tonic."

I pull out and head toward the motel signs lazily turning above the street. We pass under a fluttering banner saying WELCOME SHRINERS.

"Stop blubbering, Edith, and pull over. No reservations, no room. I'm hungry and I'm tired, in that order."

I'm not blubbering. I feel sorry for myself. When I feel sorry for myself my eyes water and my nose runs. That's all.

"How was I supposed to know the Shriners have taken over the world? Just HOW do I predict that?" I smack the steering wheel for emphasis. "It's too late to drive on. We'll eat somewhere and sleep in the car."

"You should have reserved a room. A simple phone call." Mother breaks "simple" into two distinct syllables like those TV preachers with the phony hair. Simmm-pulll "I'm an old lady. Old ladies don't sleep in cars."

"Gimme a break, okay? We'll park at the hotel, under the lights. If we lock the doors and cover up we'll be fine."

I pull into the Banff Springs Hotel and check for a gap in the cars parked in the lot. Most of the vehicles have backed into the yellow outlined spaces so I do the same, guiding the Mercedes between a motorhome and a shiny silver Volvo.

"Let's have a nice supper, Mum. You'll feel better when you've eaten." We leave the car and walk through the dusk into the massive building.

⚞

We return, defeated in the darkness. The shutting of both doors brackets the silence in the car. It doesn't last long.

"If you hadn't dallied over ice cream with that man we would've been seated in the dining room," I say, petulantly.

"We didn't have a reservation," she retaliates. "It had nothing to do with dallying."

"Of course," I add, "if they had known your hormones were running rampant, they would have made an exception."

"Stuff it, Edith."

"And the Coffee Shop closed for renovations? In September? Unbelievable."

"It's your fault," she charges. "No organizational skills."

I throw the box of candy into her lap and thrust a bottle

at her. "Just eat it and shut up."

"Don't you talk to your Mother like that."

"I'm sorry, but you're getting on my nerves."

"Let's have a nice supper, shall we?" she mocks in a sing-song voice. "Reeses Pieces and warm Cream Soda is not my idea of dinner."

"Do you want to join the Shriners in the Banquet Hall, Mother? I can dress you in a fez. Pull it right down over your wizened little body and throw you in." She's sucking her gold tooth. *Now I've done it.* "Listen, Mum," I hasten to add, "I'm sorry about this evening, okay? When we're through with this stuff I'll get a quart of peaches from the back seat. There should be some old plastic spoons in the glove compartment. That'll keep the wolves away 'til morning." *Why am I always apologizing? Sorry I have never lived up to your expectations, like Verna. Sorry I still don't have a husband and two-point-four children. Sorry this. Sorry that.*

She finds a spoon for herself and a spear-shaped swizzle stick for me. When open, the jar releases the warm aroma of brandy. I hand it to Mum and she plunges in the spoon but the peach halves slide off and in her frustration she breaks the plastic against the side of the sealer. She then uses the handle to pierce the evasive fruit, holding it dripping over the open roadmap she's using as a tablecloth. I successfully stab with my swizzle sword. The overproof brandy she smuggled across the border should preserve this crop for eternity. It was decisively overkill. Heady stuff.

We share the jar harmoniously, Mother and I. Equal portions. One for me, one for her. It works well until we reach five, then we forget whose turn it is.

"Hey, lady, you're scoffing an extra, extra peach." *I notice things like that.* "I'm a high school graduate, I can count. We are at six. I remember succinctly. Six. Succinctly ... six."

"Edith, you're pissed," says Mother.

"How 'bout you? You're looking sorta fuzzy yourself, slumped in the corner." I drain half the juice and pass the rest on.

"I am merely peached," she sniffs, tipping the bottle, head back. She waits for the last of the juice to meander down the sides.

"This promises to be a nice holiday ... " I titter, "if we ever get out of the parking lot." That must be the funniest thing I've ever said because we kick our feet and hold our stomachs as we rock. We fight to catch our breath.

"This is like the fun we had when you girls were little," Mum says when she gains control.

"It is?" I only recall what seem like inconsequential things like slug racing while camping two weeks in the rain. Or Dad relentlessly teasing Mum she couldn't hit the side of a barn with the .22 rifle and Mother saying, "Gimme the bloody gun" — aiming at the target and firing off what was in the clip in rapid succession. Each shot left a neat hole in the bulls-eye. She handed the gun back to my father and said, "Can I finish my book now, Grafton?"

"'member the time yer father took you 'n' Verna water-skiin'?" she reminisces, resting her head against the seat back.

It took me a minute to recall the event. "Yeah, now I remember. Verna went first and did it perfectly. As usual, firs' time. I didn't wanna get on water-skis. No desire, but ..."

"... but yer father insisted."

"Said if li'l Verna could do it, I could. Piece-a-cake, right? Took me three tries to surface. Never quite made it, did I? Ended up bein' a hundred-yard douche."

"Verna was just more stupple," says Mum.

"Stupple?" I question. "Stupple?"

"Yeah, stupple. Athe-letic. Your dad said she was his sports car and you were his ... what was it he called you?"

"... his Mack truck?"

"His Cadillac."

"He called me his Cadillac?" I say with surprise.

"Yup, his Cadillac," says Mum emphatically, fanning her skirt to cool her legs.

"That because I'm big and obsolete?"

"No, Edie-pie," she says, putting her warm sticky hand on my arm, "'cause you were quality ... luxury."

"He said that? Really?"

"Really," declares Mother. "You're the Cadillac kind," she says, closing the conversation.

Where was I when these compliments were being flung about? Dad had been a good car salesman and a huggable father in a detached sort of way, but according to Mother, not such a great husband. In his later years, his Alzheimer's progressed undiagnosed as he wandered into other beds, returning home as if his absence had been no more than a trip to the store for cigarettes. Mother hadn't understood it then, nor does she now, but called him a philanderer, a wolf, a ...

"Libertine," I blurt, remembering aloud.

"What?" asks Mum.

"I said 'libertine'. Such a good word, Mum. Wonder if I can work it into a Sears ad?"

"From 'The King and I'?" she asks, breaking into a tremulous soprano, "Libertine. And while we're on the subject, sire ..."

"I'm gonna get our stuff from the back." I hear her advancing through the song fearlessly as I lift the trunk lid.

"... there are certain goings-on around this place, that I wish to tell you, I do not admire. I do not like polygamy, or even ..."

The sounds from the hotel drift enticingly across the night. Sounds of people with rooms, of people who have eaten a proper meal. I gather an armload of green plastic garbage bags, shirts, a slip. I lean against the car and breath the cool air. The brandy has created clouds of cotton wool in my head. My eyes burn.

"I'll hold the bags at the top," I instruct, after re-entering the car. "You crank up the window. That'll keep it in place. Take the pillowcase off your pillow. We'll need it as a curtain."

"We'll roast with the windows up. It's already too hot. We'll be two grease spots on the seat in the morning."

"I'll crack the vents a little," I promise.

The green plastic bags hang in place on the side windows, blocking our neighbours' view. The street lamp casts an orange glow through the half slip dangling from the sun visor on my side. The bottom of the blue shirt on Mother's visor is held onto the dash with her book. There'll be no reading in bed for her tonight. The tied bundle of kindling barricades the rear window. We each release the reclining seat backs, then lie stiffly, arms folded across our midsections, blinking into the artificial noon.

"G'night," Mother says with great expectations.

"'Night." I hear a train mourning its passage. Mother has the hiccups. And either my legs are too long or this car is too short.

"Edith (hic), I have to whiz."

"Jeez, Mum, you're like a little kid. Go in the hotel."

"Come with me," she demands, lifting the garbage bag curtain. "It was your idea to have Cream Soda."

As we direct ourselves down an empty hotel corridor a voice echoes from behind. "Hey! Hey, youse two." A cadaverous man in a brown security uniform lolls against the door frame. The pants clear his black shoes exposing luminous white ankles.

"What th' hell is that?" I whisper, looking back.

"Looks (hic) like Ichabod Crane," said Mum, too loudly.

"Whadda youse doin' in here? Don'cha know it's restricted?" He advances, confidently chewing his gum in time with his walking.

"Restricted to what, young man?" says Mother huffy-like. She pulls erect, managing to be eye level with his elbow. He makes a face and fans the air, repelling her boozy breath.

"No broads allowed, eh. Shriners are initiating new guys. Secret stuff." His hand covers Mother's shoulder, turning her toward the door. "Youse gotta go."

Mother ducks beneath the extended fingers. "Hands off, Buster. If they knew how you were treating us, you'd be in dee-ee-eep shit." She picks up her skirt in both hands, raising the hem to above her knees, swishing it provocatively. "This lady and I are the entertainment. Tell him, honey." She elbows me.

"Uhh ... uhhh ..."

"She's a little slow now, but when her motor's running she's dynamite. Tell him, honey." Mother edges down the hallway, away from the guard.

"Ahh ... Ahhhh ..." I try to keep up.

"Now, you long, tall drink of water, we gotta get our (hic) feathers on. Mum's the word to the boys in there." She smiles at him and does a bump and grind. "Edith," she hisses, indicating the door with her thumb, "move your tail."

Those words have goaded me into action before and they have the same effect now. I follow her into the bathroom. We collapse against the door, with our legs crossed, laughing. It cures her hiccups.

"Did you hear him?" I ask when I catch my breath. "Said he's seen better strippers at a wallpaper convention."

While Mum's in the cubicle I sneak a look out the door and down the passageway. The guard is waiting at the exit, arms crossed.

"He's still out there," I relate. "Now what?"

"Well, we need a few feathers. So, let's take off our clothes, rip the toilet paper into long streamers ... stuff the ends into our underwear and flutter into the hallway. Those horny Shriners are waiting." We screech into hysterics. "Uh oh, won't work," she says. "Toilet paper's in little squares."

"Then we'll have to sneak out."

"How 'bout we leave through that window above the radiator? You boost me up, then follow."

"I can't fit through that little space," I point out.

"Hey, trust me — I'm a mother."

She's positioned on the sill, head and shoulders thrust out the open window. Kicking her feet clear, she inches outward, beautifully balanced, oblivious to the guard entering the restroom.

As the guard strides up, the only part showing is her legs from the red lace garter, down. I hold the empty patent leather pumps of a middle-aged woman who is teetering on the brink of a bathroom window, and I laugh until the tears drip off my chin. I ... can't ... help ... it.

He grabs both her ankles, replacing the stockinged feet on the sill. I hope Verna will send bail money. Mum turns to complain, thinking it's me wrestling her in, then sees the brown uniform.

"Oh, thank you," she coos. "I was getting a little air and I extended myself a teensy bit too far. You're so strong."

He stands Mother upright on the floor.

I hand her the shoes then wipe my eyes on the endless towel hanging from the dispenser. The guard stands fists on hips looking at us.

"Make a run for it, Edith. You're still young. Save yourself," she cries, flinging her hand to her forehead dramatically.

"Forget it, Mum." I sit on the edge of the sink and examine my nails.

"Youse ladies are to come with me. You're up to no good." He grabs Mother's arm then reaches for me.

"Be careful," I tell him, "she has a heart condition." I look her in the eye. "Don't you, Mum?"

She suddenly thumps her fingers over her chest and gasps for air.

I push him aside. "See? See what you've done?" The poor guy looks confused. Mother gropes blindly for the wall and leans against it, panting like an obscene caller.

"Want a doctor or sumthin'?" he asks, fanning her with his hat. In the harsh bathroom light I notice his semi-transparent moustache and healed acne scars.

I pat Mother's cheek. "Does this hotel have a first aid kit?" He bobs his head, mouth open. "Well, go get it."

"I dunno." He replaces the hat on his $6.00 haircut. "Youse might be foolin'."

Mother groans convincingly.

"Does that look like fooling?" I say, prodding him towards the door.

"Okay. Okay. It'll take me a few minutes." He skitters, feet slipping on the tiles as he exits.

"That's all the time we'll need, Sonny," says Mum brightly,

returning from the dead.

There's now clear access down the hallway. I signal to Mother and she minces along on tiptoe over the worn carpeting. Outside, pools of darkness hide our unsteady flight through the parking lot. Mother teeters in her high heels. She uses her hand as a guide to round our car, her fingers leaving tracks in the dust. It's cooler now so I remove two sweaters from the trunk before getting into the Mercedes. The rent-a-cop, ever alert, is scanning the parking area for two suspicious miscreants, but he doesn't leave the security of the building.

"Put this on, Mum, so you don't get cold. Can't have your heart acting up again." She has trouble finding the arm holes. We lock ourselves in as we prepare to settle down. I look over at her as she tucks her legs under her dress, then removes her earrings, putting them in the ashtray with the gum wrappers. "Who are you?" I question.

"Go to sleep, Edith."

"Are you really my mother?"

"No. The woman didn't know how to live, so I took over her body, such as it is." She retrieves her pillow from the back seat. "Now go to sleep. It's been a long day."

A raucous chorus of male voices issues final farewells as the patrons depart the hotel. Shoes stumble over the pavement. Voices stop nearby. I lift the plastic bag to check into the side-view mirror but nobody looks back.

During the restless noisy night I dream there's a tapping, tapping at the window and a plaintive little voice calling "Dixie? Dixie?" A door closes with a click. It's finally quiet. Can't even hear Mother's nose whistle as she sleeps.

▲

I'd raise my wrist to look at my watch but I can't find my arm. Everything hurts. I believe something has nested in my mouth. Mother looks remarkable.

"How'd you do that?" I mumble.

"What, dear?" she asks, smiling.

"Get dressed without me hearing?" She's wearing her purple jogging suit and runners. And goldfish earrings. And lipstick.

Rolling down her window she releases the green plastic bag, which she folds neatly into a square. The shirt from the visor is also folded onto her lap.

"It's going to be a wonderful day," she proclaims. "Just look at that blue sky above the trees."

"Mother? You didn't go back to the hotel, did you?" I lift my plastic bag to check for police cars.

"Fate is an amazing thing," she says, very self-satisfied.

"What the hell does that mean?" I irritably yank at the half-slip-and-garbage-bag curtain.

"Want a comb, Edith?" she asks cheerfully, holding hers out.

My hair looks like it needs a building permit. The lost arm tingles from fingers to shoulder.

Mother folds the items I force into her lap and looks congenial as she passes it all back to me in a neat stack. "Put it away, that's a good girl." She is humming something familiar.

"You're pretty chipper for someone who slept in a car all night." I scrunch on my shoes then open the door. The mountain air which should be sweet and crisp is choking with exhaust fumes. The motorhome next to us sits idling. I open our trunk and throw in the paraphernalia. Mother's paisley print dress is balled around her slip. The seamed nylons she spent endless hours shopping for are wadded into one of her patent leather pumps.

The driver of the motorhome steps on the gas to rev up the lagging motor, releasing more toxic fog.

"Jerk," I say as I slam the lid.

He slides open the window to reveal a chubby arm with

stubby little sausage fingers. "Hi there, Edith. Great day, huh?" He puts the vehicle into gear. The aluminum beast lumbers from its lair with *that* bumper sticker, IF THIS MOTORHOME'S A-ROCKIN' — DON'T COME KNOCKIN'. He toots the horn as he drives away. A familiar red lace garter sways from the fringed shade in the rear window.

"M-u-u-u-ther-r-r!" I lunge at the car door yanking it open. "I know how you did it!" I yell.

She's sitting with fingers entwined on her lap, feet demurely crossed. "Did what, dear?"

"YOU KNOW WHAT!"

"I have no idea what you're talking about, Edith. Please keep your voice down. People are sleeping."

"First night out and you spend it with some strange man. How could you?" I protest. "He looks like the Pillsbury Dough Boy." She smiles as if the world is her oyster.

I crank the car onto the roadway heading for town. "Three hours after I turned twelve you cautioned me 'Edith, keep your knees together. Edith, keep your legs crossed.' Took me years to figure out what the hell you were talking about. When I did, there was nobody interested anyway." It was unusual not to be interrupted, so I continue. "Now look at YOU. What have you got to say for yourself?"

She's humming — clicking the ends of her thumbnails together keeping time to the music. She rests her head against the back of the seat, humming contentedly all the way to town.

The tires scuff against the curb near Lovechild's Diner. The other cars parked in front I take as a good indicator of a decent place to eat. The steamy windows hold a blue neon OPEN sign. I pocket the keys. She's now whistling through her teeth, annoying me no end.

"You can damn well sit here by yourself."

My seatbelt catches in the closing car door, the buckle dangling just above the road. To hell with it. Inside, the café smells of fresh coffee. I find the washroom and see, reflected in the mirror, my wrinkled clothes and puffy eyes. I should get my makeup bag from the trunk, but I refuse to go back out. After some attempted restoration, I abandon all hope, leaving the bathroom mirror behind. Best thing to do is find a table and order breakfast.

Under a greasy baseball cap, a flushed face pops up from the kitchen behind the counter. "Grabba seat, lady, the girl will be right with ya." A piece of machinery whirs in his hands.

I take a chair facing the door. On every wall are dog-eared posters of Diana Ross wearing fly-specked, sequined gowns. Album covers are permanently embedded in the yellowing plaster ceiling. Contained within a glass frame, a card attached to a lipsticked paper hanky explains: DIANA ROSS' KLEENEX, SEATTLE 1967. The place is a shrine. The Supremes ooze through the corner speakers. Propped on the table, a 45-record with a tatty menu glued to one side; the other holds the original label with "Love Child" in worn gold lettering.

"Must have named the place after the record," I say out loud, reading the menu on my lap.

"Mucho smart, lady." Unfortunately, in my line of vision are a pair of feet encased in black leotards and curling sandals.

"Charleen. Charleen. Charleen."

"Where's the old lady? Out haunting houses?" Charleen's holding a pot of coffee like a pistol. She hooks her finger inside the rim of my cup and pulls it toward her.

"Didn't take you long to acquire employment, Charleen. You must have very marketable skills."

"Don't take that shitty attitude with me," she wheezes. "You left me sucking the hind tit in Spuzzum." She pours coffee until it overflows the cup. "I caught a bitch of a cold, thanks to you," she sniffs resonantly.

I gingerly lift the cup to position three serviettes on the

saucer. The stain radiates like a muddy sunrise. Charleen leaves my side to charm the other diners. Hunched over the cup, I swoop down to sip at the rim. It's not very good but it beats the pants off Cream Soda. I watch the door for Mother. She's taking her sweet time.

An ancient clock, bearing no resemblance to Diana Ross, reads 7:40. At the side of the clock, encased in a lighted pink frame is a series of cards which rotate and flop over. They advertise local merchants and their wares. *Tony's skate sharpening ... Sonja's scalp treatment ... Abdul's English Fish and Chips.* I adjust my watch to match Alberta time. The door opens but it's not Mother, just a working stiff in cork boots wanting his thermos filled as he heads for the jobsite.

So, let her sit there and suffer. See if I care. I re-read the record-menu. Charleen leans against the counter, arms crossed, daring me to order. "Excuse me, Miss," I call, just short of snapping my fingers.

She checks over her shoulder as the owner raises his head to my summons. She slouches to the table, sandals patting the flowered linoleum. "Whaddya want?" she asks, hand on hostile hip.

"You want to keep this job, Charleen, or shall we go a round or two?"

"Just gimme your order," she grouses. The owner wipes his beefy hands across the front of his apron as he approaches. Charleen smiles and says grandly, "Yes, madam, it is a lovely day. How may I serve you?"

"I'll have the Number Eight Special, please. Make that two. My dear mother will be joining me."

The owner scowling over his potato-size nose, reverses his baseball cap.

"Two Number Eights, Bruno ... please," chirps Charleen on her way to the till where departing customers are impatiently jingling change.

Bruno watches Charleen briefly then turns to ask, "What's goin' on? She botherin' ya?"

"No ... lovely girl. Been here long?"

"Yeah, started last night." He scuffs back to the kitchen to work on two Number Eights.

I leave the table to check Mother. Clearing a little circle in the window condensation lets me see her sitting exactly as I left her, except that her eyes are closed and she's smiling. *Damn her, anyway.* I stomp to the car.

I rap on the pane next to her ear — with a quarter. That gets her attention. That self-satisfied smile dissolves and her hand slaps over her heart. I motion for her to roll down the glass. As she does, she's breathing hard, glaring at me.

"You coming or not?"

"Not!" She winds up the window.

I stoop over and squash my nose against the glass. "Mother, I have ordered your breakfast."

"Eat it yourself."

"But it's your favourite," I wheedle. "Bruno's Number Eight Special. And coffee slopped into the saucer just the way you like it." The car door creaks open and one foot tentatively feels for the curb.

She enters royally, back rigid, looking neither right nor left. That lasts until the waitress crosses her path. "Isn't that," she rudely waves a finger in her direction, "what's-her-name?"

"Charleen? Our Freeway Fruitfly? The Handmaiden of the Highway? One and the same. Table's over here," I direct.

"How did you manage to find the only place in town that would hire her?" Mother wipes the orange leatherette seat before sitting.

"Well, I thought it might be nice to see a friendly face and Charleen came to mind. You have your friends, I have mine."

"Will your sniping be setting the trend for the whole day?"

"Probably." I slip two napkins under Mother's cup as I see Charleen's perilous advance with two plates on her arm and more coffee in hand.

"Two Specials." She drops the platters onto the table and shoves them before us. "Would you like cutlery or you just gonna use your claws?" she asks, pouring coffee that weeps over the rim.

THE CADILLAC KIND

Mother has little ridges in her jaws when she clamps them.
I watch the ridges pulse. Her face puckers, pleating around
her nose. The lips work, then deliver a reluctant laugh. *It
could have gone either way.* In the middle of the table,
Charleen plunks a tumbler holding stainless steel utensils.
Haute cuisine.

After mopping the last of the egg with toast, we sit back,
sated. We have done justice to Bruno's breakfast. I signal
Charleen to return with coffee.

"Just a half, please," I request, pushing my plate aside to
reach the cup.

"How did you manage to get to Banff?" Mother asks the
girl.

"That truck stop where you gave me the boot? Next guy
in picks me up. Real friendly. Good sound system, too.
Blauplunkt with dual speakers. Bringing stuff right here to
Bruno's. How 'bout that for shithouse luck?" Before leaving
our table, she smacks down the bill. Holding it stationary
are four green mints of questionable age.

"Edith, remember in school, first day back, you always
had to write 'How I Spent My Summer Vacation'?"

I nod.

"Want to hear how I spent mine, last night?"

"Not particularly," I reply, reaching for my wallet.

"It's not what you think," she counters, playing with the
mints.

"Can you imagine how many other people have done the
same thing?"

"Spent the night with Walter?" she asks, startled.

"No, fondled those mints." She releases them into the
ashtray.

"Walter and I had a perfectly lovely evening."

"You're gonna tell me anyway, aren't you?"

"We played crib. I was up seventy-five cents at one point.
He made tea and served smoked oysters on cute little fish
crackers."

"We all know what the oysters are for, don't we? Is that
how you lost your garter?"

37

"Hey! It was a souvenir. He was lonely. Walter just wanted a little companionship."

"Walter? Walter? Did you catch his last name? In case we have to notify the clinic?"

"Muckle."

"Muckle? Ma ... ha ... ha ... kull?" I laugh.

"It's a respected name in the community."

"What community, Mother?"

"Yahk."

"Walter Muckle from Yahk? It's too good."

"I know."

"What's he do for a living?"

She pauses, lowering her voice and raising one eyebrow. "He sells Fair Maidens Caerphilly."

My jaw falls. "He's a pimp? And he told you?"

"It's a joke, Edith. A cheese joke. Walter sells cheese. Fair Maiden Cheese. Caerphilly is a young Welsh cheese made from cow's milk." Mother recites her lesson well.

"So, on your first night of summer holidays, along comes some cheese salesman. Walter Muckle from Yahk. He lets you win a few hands, then he tries a few hands, wink, wink, nudge nudge, then out come the oysters, you lose the garter, and then what? No, no, don't tell me. You fuckled a Muckle."

A fine mist of coffee sprays over the table. She chokes down the remainder. "I ... did ... no ... such ... thing!"

"You didn't Muckle fu ... ?"

"Don't say it." Mother holds up her hand, warding off the interrogation. "No, I didn't."

"Oh, sorry." I say.

"Me, too," says Mother, scraping back her chair and standing. "It wasn't for lack of trying."

We're finally underway with two last minute cream cheese and bacon sandwiches sitting on the seat between us. Once we're back on the highway, I confess, "Too late for you to do anything about it now, Mum, but I felt sorry for Charleen and left a five dollar tip."

"Too late for you to do anything about it now, Edith, but I took it. That's how I paid for the sandwiches."

She snores in the corner, mouth agape, goldfish earrings swimming with the movement of the car. I wonder when she got so interesting. And so promiscuous. She wasn't like that when I was a kid.

In my younger days, my best friend Helen had a mother with a mysterious limp from a mysterious accident.

Or Gayle's mother, a native Indian, tucked her one long braid into the waistband of her pants. She smoked game meat in her backyard for the neighbours in exchange for rides to town when she needed groceries.

Our mother, Verna's and mine, walked without a falter and had ordinary short brown hair that she home-permed.

She and the neighbour, Mrs. Robertson, would often visit to sew up flour sack slips for us to wear under our navy-blue school jumpers. The red letters of the flour company never completely faded, even when the slips had dwindled into dust rags. And Mum would change her rumpled housedress for another before my father arrived home from the car lot at night. She'd tell us, "if you want to keep a marriage happy, don't wear curlers to bed and always look nice when your man comes home."

I dreaded company on a Sunday for that's when she'd probably say to the unsuspecting audience assembled on the velour couch, "Verna's going to dance for you." Then she would keep time while Verna stumbled through her ballet repertoire, curtsying to politely enthusiastic applause. Dad would ruffle Verna's hair when she was finished, and she would smile up at him, tightening her hold on his heart. In an aside to the visitors, Mother would add, "She inherited her talent, you know. I took training as a dancer." When questioned as to why she hadn't gone on to greater things, she would trace a swollen belly over her flat one and tilt her head in my direction. Eyes would shift towards me and knowing eyebrows rise. "Grafton wanted a family." She would sigh dramatically, adding, "it's now up to Verna to be the dancer." The only thing lacking in this drama was her flinging the back of her hand to her forehead and swooning onto the chesterfield. Having done her poor-me routine she would then try to shoehorn me into the social circle. "And our Edith is a fine reader. Don't slouch, dear. Read us something from the Life magazine."

I guess we can stop in Calgary so she can visit the Aunts. I'll stipulate one hour. ONE HOUR. Tea, cookies and polite conversation. I haven't seen the old girls since Grandma Joan's funeral. Must be fourteen, fifteen years ago. That's where most everyone ended up square dancing on the back lawn. Even Mum, and it was her mother they were burying. She said it was their way of throwing a wake. Dad rated a barbecue and pitchers of sangria.

"Mum, we're on the outskirts of Calgary. You wanna wake up and phone the Aunts?"

She yawns noisily and stretches. "I wasn't sleeping." After pulling her purse onto her lap, she up-ends the contents. "Somewhere in here's my address book," she claims.

"You want me to pull over at the next phone?"

"Yeah yeah, pull over. I found it."

"That's your bankbook."

"It's my address book. The account's closed so I use it for something better."

I drive next to the open doors of a phone booth near a service station. *I hope they're not home. Could be their Bingo afternoon. Two-for-One Day at the doctor's?*

Her hands wave as she speaks to someone on the other end. In that animated wave she has taken in her surroundings, the car, me, and the threat that we will be arriving on their threshold at any moment.

"They're home," she announces after hanging up, never doubting they wouldn't be. "I talked to Rhetta. She's putting on the tea."

"Let's eat our sandwiches on the way, then we can just have a cookie and leave." I push Bruno's lunch toward her.

"Edith, don't start. The old girls will be insulted if we don't spend time. After all, we're family."

"You know, I remember visiting them when I was small. They used to let me sit in their living room while they watched from the hallway. The other kids couldn't go in but I was given about three minutes. Couldn't touch those glass baubles that hung from all the lampshades. They'd let me blow on them, just a little. Soon as I puffed up my cheeks, Rhetta would lean over and coo, 'Gently, now.' They were like turkey vultures."

"They do sort of feed off one another." said Mum rebuckling the seatbelt. "Vultures is too strong a word, though. More like an orchid on a tree. Symbiotic."

"Have they always lived together? They don't even like each other, do they?" I check the glove compartment for the road map.

"Yes and no. The three sisters, Ida, Rhetta and Mums, had a house the other end of Calgary. Mums moved in with the Aunts after Pops died. Queenie and I were long gone by then. Anyway, someone decided to build a jam factory smack dab on their property. The old girls saw an opportunity to make a buck. Oh, they put on a memorable performance, from what Mums told me later. Held up their land titles and cried a lot at being 'thrown to the wolves'. The factory upped the ante and the Aunties upped the factory."

"... and the sisterly bond?"

"Oh, I guess they like one another, grudgingly. Mums once hinted that Rhetta had stolen a man from Ida Ruth. Those two had a past of some kind but I wasn't privy to the gossip. They were plain as young girls, all three of them."

"Can you remember how to get there?"

"99 Quail's Run Lane," recites Mother, not even referring to her bank book. "I never forget the address, just the route."

"Where's the map? I'll look it up."

Maps, after being used, should always be refolded along the original lines. Those creases were designed by a clean mind — no litter, no excess. Mother thinks maps should be folded Origami-like. She reduces the map to a thing that resembles the colon of a wood buffalo. The paper she crammed under her seat last night is laminated with bits of peach. The street names are glazed with brandy-laced syrup. I hold it before her scornfully.

She snatches it. "You make such an issue of things." I leave the car hearing tearing sounds and walk toward the garage.

I discover we aren't more than twenty minutes away. The newly purchased map is caressed into shape and placed in the side pocket of the door. My side. "You really want to see them?" I ask before starting out.

"I really do. They're Mums' only sisters. They're probably on their last legs. Old Granny had those three before she knew where babies came from. My mother was the oldest, then Ida, she's about eighty-six, and Rhetta, near eighty-five. We're definitely stopping."

I manoeuvre the car, trailing a cloak of dust, down their unpaved street. The house distances itself from the roadway by hunkering down in an unruly stretch of tall grass. We climb a set of cement steps. Next to them, a mailbox with somebody's version of a quail painted on the side. The tiger lilies the bird stands in form the number ninety-nine. This is the sole house on the block. Only the road holds back the advance of bordering wild meadows.

"Is this for real?" The neglected exterior of the house made me think the place might have had a previous life as Bates' Motel.

Two elderly women try simultaneously to get out the door onto the verandah. They butt hips and press sharpened elbows into the other's unprotected parts.

"Those girls never could get along," says Mother unnecessarily.

"Who's the stocky one with the hearing aid? Rhetta or Ida?"

"Ida Ruth."

Now free of the doorway, Ida Ruth propels Rhetta sideways with the flat of her hand. Lurching forward, Rhetta stops the momentum by seizing the column at the top of the stairs. She throws both arms around the pillar, like a virgin resisting a sacrificial plunge.

"How nice to see you, Dixie." We pick our way over the crumbling cement sidewalk. "Ida, sweet, it's Dixie and umm, uhh ..." burbles Rhetta, releasing her hold on the support.

"Edith!" prompts Ida. "We went over it minutes ago, remember?"

The two sisters link arms. They advance until the toes of their runners hang over the top step of the porch.

"Lovely seeing the two of you again," says Mum, looking up. She almost sounds sincere.

I yell toward Ida, "Morning, Auntie," hoping she hears. We're advised to come inside.

After the brilliance of the morning, the interior of the house looks like a grotto. The Aunts are urging us on but we both wait for our eyes to become accustomed to the shadows.

"Take your shoes off." Sounds like the big one, Ida.

We lean against the wall for balance while we untie shoelaces.

"Leave 'em on, sweets," contradicts the skinny one, Rhetta.

I look to Mother for direction. She flips one shoe into a corner and follows the Aunts, tickie, pat, tickie, pat. She walks with a nautical list. I follow suit.

We proceed single file into the smothering interior of the parlour.

"Which side do you want to sit on, hers or mine?" asks Ida, fists jammed into her substantial hips.

"Uhh, which is which?" I judiciously inquire.

"My gawd, any idiot could tell. Look around," Ida replies sharply.

Two sofas square off midpoint in the high-ceilinged room. At either end bevelled pane windows, each exhibiting its owners fondness in draperies. Each half of the room reflects opposing tastes, stoutly defended.

"Sister Ida and I have come to an understanding. Her side, the PLAIN one, is beyond the yellow marker on the floor. Ida stays in her half and I stay in mine." She plumps a ruffled chintz pillow on the velveteen couch. "We like to think of them as our own little kingdoms, don't we, sweets?"

Ida picks up the story. "Rhetta is supposed to bring her company, IF she has any, through the OTHER door at the end of the room. HER doorway entirely," she waves. "Seeing as you used MY door to enter, you can use HER door to leave."

That sets the house rules in order.

"Why two of everything?"

"SHE," points Ida, "wanted a window and bric-a-brac."

"SHE," says Rhetta indicating with her elbow, "wanted a window and the bleakness of Jane Eyre."

"So, you both wanted a window and you divided the room. I get it."

"You should have noticed that right off, Edith. Silly you," Mother chides.

Minutes later, Ida pulls the grey plastic knob from her ear, dangling the device from its cord. "Crap. Pure unadulterated crap." She waggles a finger into the vacated ear. "Make up your mind who you're having tea with. It's getting cold."

It's a careful tea. The silver tray, polished to a faultless bloom, is on Rhetta's table.

"That is a beautiful service, Aunt Rhetta. Was it the family's?" I say, making conversation.

"Yes, sweetie. Unfortunately it goes to the ELDEST sister. Now that Joan is gone, that makes Ida Ruth the oldest by a mile. She doesn't like to fuss with polishing and the like so I have custodial rights."

"As usual," interrupts Ida, "Rhetta arrived too late to collect the goodies. Always one step behind." Her smile is like the zipper on an old travel bag. "More Earl Grey?" she asks, motioning Rhetta to pour.

I feel I have to balance things, even them out — like this room. "The cookies are very nice. Did you bake them, Aunt Ida?" I broach tentatively, "or, or Aunt Rhetta?" I should just shut up as Mother has done.

"I don't bake."

I address Rhetta, and take another. "They are unusual."

"Help yourself, my sweet. I volunteer a few hours a week

down at the old jam factory. Remember, Dixie, where we used to live? They have a camp for so-called anti-social teens. Those girls can be so adorable," she smiles. "Why sometimes they steal the teeth right out of my mouth and skid them across the linoleum. It makes them laugh to see me feeling for them under the bookcase. I do enjoy bringing gladness into their hearts."

"… and the cookies?" I know I'm going to be sorry I asked, after eating three, maybe four.

"Oh, yes, the cookies," she continues. "Well, those cheerful young ladies bake for the staff and volunteers each week. Isn't that thoughtful? They won't touch a-one just so we have enough to take home. Makes me teary just thinking about it."

Most mothers wouldn't laugh at a time like this. Willie Nelson's would hustle him out to a stomach pump. She'd worry and console him. But not mine.

Ida re-inserts the earpiece, not wanting to miss a thing. "Bullshit!" she explodes a moment later, sailing the word on a fine mist of saliva.

"Say 'bullshirt' when company's here, Ida, please. It's more refined." Rhetta smiles at us apologetically.

"THANK YOU FOR TEA, AUNT IDA."

"Why the hell do you insist on yelling at me, girl? I'm not deaf," she bristles.

"You keep adjusting your hearing aid, so I thought …"

"Hearing aid at MY age? It's a radio," she says pulling the plug from her ear, and setting the equipment on the table. "I'm TRYING to listen to the phone-in talk show. Stupid woman from Edmonton just said something nice about the Prime Minister."

Rhetta, ignoring the outburst, replaces her cup on the bone china saucer. "So, loves, who gets the top?"

"Top of what, Auntie?" I politely inquire.

"There's a bottom and a top, as Ida explained to your mother over the phone. Both have their advantages. Actually, some people prefer one to another. So that's why I'm asking. Who gets the top?"

"Top of WHAT, Auntie?" This has come full circle.

Rhetta sadly shakes her head as if sympathizing with the parent of a backward child. She leans forward, a hand covering each knobby knee, to explain yet again. "Who … gets … the top … bunk?"

"Oh, we're not staying," I say with relief, looking to my travelling companion for affirmation. She's suddenly found dust on her only shoe.

"We wouldn't hear otherwise," says Rhetta. "Isn't that right, Ida Ruth?" Ida grunts a reply. "See, ducky, Ida would be crushed if you two didn't stay after we made arrangements."

"Excuse me a moment." I cross the void, and cosy up to Mother. "What do you know about this?" I whisper fiercely in her ear.

"It's a good opportunity for you to rest, dear," she says, edging away.

"What else?" I demand.

"You could have a bubble bath and change your clothes?"

"What else?"

"We're here for the night?"

"What *else*?"

"That's it! One night."

I address the Aunts who are fidgety, being excluded from the altercation. "Mother's advancing age sometimes plays little tricks," I explain. "She has these black holes in her mind where information gets sucked in but doesn't come out."

The aunts tut-tut. Mother picks at her gold tooth and swings her foot.

"I didn't realize we had been invited to stay over," I reveal, clutching my purse to my bosom. "Much as we'd like to, we couldn't possibly. We have to go." I'm the only one standing. "Thanks for tea."

A sudden wheeze from Aunt Rhetta exposes perfect plastic teeth in what could be a smile, but beneath her rhinestone glasses, tears zig-zag down crevices as deeply etched as cut glass. She buries her face in her hands, sobbing noisily.

Ida rolls her eyes as she picks up the dishes, stacking cups every which way. They're toted to the kitchen on the silver tray. Mother's mouth pinches and those small calibre eyes shoot live ammunition my way. "See … what … you've … done?" she admonishes, moving to console Aunt Rhetta with a friendly arm across her quaking shoulder. "Break an old lady's heart, Edith. Shame!"

Why am I fighting Walter Muckle? He can have her. "We'd love to stay, Auntie," I lie. "Just thought it might be too much trouble for you."

Her wailing stops immediately and she smiles. "Lovely, sweets." She hops up, pattering towards the kitchen. "I'll go tell Sister."

I turn on Mother. "YOU are getting the top," I promise through clenched teeth.

Mum relaxes while I bring in the suitcases. The Aunts have put away my shoe, the one Ida insisted I leave at the doorway. I'm sure a rumpled, wild-eyed woman with one shoe, tromping up and down the sidewalk in front of *this* house would not raise an eyebrow.

As I re-enter, Mother requests the basket of dried flowers to show the Aunts.

Back to the car.

They want to see her golf clubs.

Sure they do!

Would I be a very nice daughter and take another teensie walk to bring in her peaches? Mum and Rhetta bob and smile and promise "last time".

I wonder how they got to be *her* peaches. I bought them, slipped the skins, made the syrup, sterilized the jars, had the cooker on the boil when she waltzed in, in her crisp walking shorts, mentioning how frazzled I looked. Her contribution was the smuggled brandy which she poured with a heavy hand into each jar just before sealing.

"Like an armload of kindling, Mother, while I'm out there?"

"We don't need a fire today, sweets," says Rhetta fanning her throat with a *Reader's Digest*.

"But Mother can tell you how she split each and every

stick by hand … using only a butter knife."

She sucks her tooth in warning as she rises from the couch, her chin leading the way, finger aimed at my heart.

Three women with the same flinty little eyes means I'm out-numbered. I don't turn my back on them as I leave.

After fetching and carrying comes the time to move the suitcases left in the hallway. As I climb the stairs a close, cloying smell of lemon oil emanates from the burnished wooden banisters.

I take a few minutes to lay my clothes out on the bottom bunk.

When I return downstairs, Mum and the Aunts have left the living room and are sitting around the dining-room table. Three half-empty sealers of fruit nest on tatted doilies, a numbered paper stuck to each front. On a count of four, they each pierce a peach, and lower it dripping into a flowered fruit nappy. Like connoisseurs they judge for taste, aroma, smoothness of flesh before passing the jar along.

I join them, aware of their flushed cheeks and lustrous eyes.

"What are we doing?" I ask, trying to be sociable.

"Seeing whose is best," says Ida, wiping her sticky mouth on her thumb.

"Aren't all home-canned peaches pretty well the same?" The cracking of vertebrae sounds as three necks crank at my indiscretion.

Mother's mouth opens then closes and she looks a bit lost. "Funny, I forget what I was going to say."

"You were probably going to say, 'will the maker of jar number two … COME ON DOWN!'" says Rhetta, raising the glass bottle on high, tinging the sides with her fork.

Ida swipes at it. "That's not your jar."

"'Tis, too." Rhetta clasps it to her chest, plugging the open end with her chin. "Mine has the rum, and this is definitely RUM. Cap'n Morgan. Rum. Tum tum."

"Mine's sherry, and that smells like sherry, you dotty old fart."

The sisters glare at one another.

"Girls, girls," Mother intones senatorially. "I have a nose for such things. Giz 'em here." I wonder if the UN could use another Goodwill Ambassador? She aligns the three containers, then lingers over each in turn, inhaling the bouquet. "Jar number one has the sherry, BUT, just to be sure ..." The bayonetted peach glows round side up in the Royal Albert dish. Mother incises the unblemished flesh. "Sherried perfection."

"So, mine's the best? I win," Ida bellows triumphantly. "No contest."

"I didn't say you win. I only said it was sherry. Actually, I prefer my own," says Mother, straying onto dangerous ground.

"And I pick MINE," says Ida Ruth. "Some contest!" She scowls, turning her back to the table.

I stand, under the assumption that it garners some authority to be above the rabble. "Ladies, ladies. You're ALL winners in your own way." If Mother is to be an Ambassador for Peace then I will be Speaker of the House. "We're among friends. Kiss and make up."

"Siddown and shaddup," cries the trio.

Finally, something they agree on.

During the silence that breaks out, I gather up the peach remains and syrupy dishes.

"Got anything planned for the rest of the day, Aunt Rhetta?" I call from the kitchen.

"Yes, dearie, as a matter of fact, I do. You two are in for a real big surprise," she bubbles in a rush of words. "Guess what happens later this afternoon? Just guess." She claps her hands enthusiastically beneath her chin.

"Afternoon delight?" I volunteer, returning to the table. "A madcap threesome with Walter?" I'm sorry as soon as I say it. Well, sort of.

"Edith Ann Flood!" says the voice of doom about to deliver a charge.

"You were saying, Auntie?" I butt in, ignoring Mother..

"Who's Walter?" she asks, leaning forward intently, awaiting an answer.

My chance to gain points. "He's a friend of Mother's. LOVE-ly man. Has a motorhome with six speakers. Runs about the country selling cheese."

"Oh," says a disappointed Rhetta. "Dixie, are you still guessing?"

"Apple dunking? Alligator wrestling? Acrobatics?" Mother is gamely working her way through the alphabet. "Aerobics?"

Ida intercedes. "We've got BOWLING. That's what!"

Rhetta sinks to the table deflated. "You were s-o-o-o close, Dixie."

"You two can come if you can keep up," Ida challenges.

"I think we'll manage. Bowled a number of years ago." *No sense telling them about my ball bounding across three busy lanes and punching a little, hardly noticeable hole in the wall.* "How 'bout you, Mum?"

"Well, I was pretty good at it when Grafton and the guys from the car lot had a Bowling League."

"Tell them about the time you won a turkey," say I, trying to get back on her good side.

"We bowled every second Tuesday," she relates. "The guys would go every Tuesday but every second Tuesday the wives or girlfriends were invited. There was one fellow, Tommy?" She looks to me for prompting, but I shrug not knowing his last name. "Tommy Merridew, that's it, who brought both." She sits back, crossing her legs. "Brought his wife AND his girlfriend. Every second Tuesday."

"No! Tell me more," coaxes Rhetta.

"Tommy always sat between them. He'd chat them up until it was his turn to bowl, then he'd check over his shoulder to make sure they didn't close the space he'd just left. Bowled real quick, Tommy did."

"What happened to the women? The wife and girlfriend?" asks Ida, reluctantly caught up in the story.

"When Tommy got up to bowl, they'd swear at one another. They'd start with one word insults. By the time Tommy lobbed two balls down the alley those girls were almost at blows. Tommy tried his damnedest to get strikes so he could get right back."

"And ... ?"

Mother pauses dramatically. "He made the Provincial Team. Then the National. He got promoted to Head Office on his bowling ability. The women went with him. He needed them both to keep up his score."

It isn't the epic tale of Mother winning the turkey but it tickles the Aunts. They slouch in their chairs, resting elbows on the oval table. Then Ida pushes back, lamenting that it's her turn to do dishes, leaving Rhetta and Mother to discuss the merits of dried flowers. I feel it's safe to head upstairs for a bath and change of clothes.

I love rooms with slanted ceilings, so Anne-of-Green-Gable-ish. Waxed hardwood floor, cabbage-sized pink roses on the wallpaper, hooked rug made with confetti coloured rags. The ornate metal bunk-bed squeaks as I sit on it. My shoe is pulled off and stashed beneath the bed. When I stretch out, the soft goosedown pillows bunch up around my ears muffling the conversation from below. Outside the open window is a poplar tree with starlings. Nearby, a horse neighs.

⬥

"Come on Edith, get up. Time to go bowling."

"Go away."

"The Aunts are waiting."

"Gimme four more hours."

"Move it!"

"Go without me."

"MOVE IT!"

My feet hit the floor. "Yes, sir, Sergeant-Major, SIR."

"That's better," she says, awarding me a snappy salute.

"You have bags under your eyes, dear," says Auntie when I finally descend the stairs.

"Thanks for calling it to my attention, Aunt Rhetta."

"Your mother thought twenty minutes was long enough. She's says you're cranky if you sleep too long."

"That luxury hasn't happened yet. I don't think I've had more than three good hours since we left Vancouver." I notice my runner has been returned. It's disgustingly clean.

"We'll leave as soon as Sister and your mother see that Alphonse gets his treat."

"Who's Alphonse?"

"Well, sweets, when we converted the basement, we took him in."

"You have a boarder?"

"So to speak."

"Alphonse lives in the basement?"

"Yes, he does."

"He certainly is quiet. I hope we haven't bothered him with our comings and goings."

"He didn't notice. Been out back on the grass."

"All this time?"

"He loves the outdoors, does Alphonse. Here they are," cries Rhetta. "Ready, Dix? Sister? It's Girls Night Out."

"Girls NIGHT out? Is this going to take forever?"

"A little bowling, Edith, a little dinner. Let's make a day of it," says Mother gaily. "We may not be through Calgary for another fifteen years." She pushes at me from behind. "Out, out."

Mum's voice rebounds against the bedroom ceiling just inches from her face.

"What did you say?" The springs in the bed above me shape to her outline.

"I said, you shouldn't have let me eat that mountain of pyrogies tonight. All those onions. All that sour cream. Why didn't you stop me?"

"I thought you were trying gastronomic suicide. Once you've been led to the trough, there's no stopping you."

"A gentle reminder would have done it."

"Mmmm."

"Edith?"

"What?" Moonlight casts long leafy poplar shadows that slip over the floor's waxed finish and seep into the cracks.

"Thanks for not laughing at the Aunts this afternoon."

"Now, why would I do that?" *Take a big breath and let it out slowly.*

"Because of those pink fluorescent slacks Rhetta wore bowling." She shifts position above me.

"Those weren't slacks, Mum. They were spandex tights. She's just so damned skinny they bagged." Even though she covers her mouth I hear her. "Shame on you," I scold. "You didn't laugh when Aunt Ida — how can I put it? — released enough methane to blow a lethal hole in the ozone."

The bed squeaks as her heels thump the mattress.

"Did you know Aunt Rhetta wore a wig?" I ask.

"Not ... til ... it ... hit the floor."

"And the shoe-rental kid calling the SPCA 'cause he thought she'd stepped on the resident cat and killed it."

We laugh until we hear a distant rapping on the walls.

"We'd better be quiet. Probably worried about waking the boarder."

"What boarder?"

"The one you met this afternoon. Alphonse."

"Alphonse won't care."

"How do you know?" I question. "Is he 'deef', as Ida would say."

"Not at all." She shifts again fighting the pyrogies. "He hears very well for a gelding."

"He's been gelded? The poor guy," I say with concern. "A wounded veteran, then?"

"A GELDING, for gawd's sake! You know, four legs, road apples, ground into dog food."

"Oh, for chrissake."

"All those onions ..."

⋏

I yawn and stretch, noticing the sun is melting into a different corner, and Mother still hasn't brought coffee. I vaguely remember her stepping on my hand as she rappelled from the top bunk. I've given her a big head start hoping she'll carry up a freshly brewed cup of mocha java. But it looks like she's a no-show.

Reluctantly I sit up. Nothing hurts. Guess I had a good sleep. Mother's bag is still open, clothes spilling onto the floor. I tug my suitcase from under the bunk and gather whatever has the least wrinkles.

My hair is so tangled I can't get my fingers through. A little Brylcreme should tame it to manageable proportions. Another advantage of getting up late, aside from the sheer luxury, is getting the bathroom to myself.

I hear the Aunts chatting below as I torpidly head downstairs after dressing.

"Morning, all," I say to the two figures sitting in the living room.

The conversation dies as I enter. Aunt Ida is on her side of the room, Aunt Rhetta opposite. "Mornin'," drones the duo, not looking up.

"What's the matter? Get up on the wrong side of the bed?"

"Nope."

"Where's Mother?"

They look at one another, then shrug their shoulders in unison.

"What does that mean?" I lean against the door frame, enjoying their little joke.

"She's gone," says Ida. "Buggered off in a motorhome."

"A motorhome? A MOTORHOME! Damn her."

"It's okay, sweets," says Rhetta fluttering over to pat my arm. "She'll be back real soon."

"She told you that?"

"Well, not exactly. Would you like tea?" she offers.

"What EXACTLY did she say?"

"Come have a nice cuppa, dear, and we'll talk."

She leads the way to the dining-room table. I slump into a chair and prop my head in my hands. Alphonse is grazing in the back yard. Aunt Ida is grazing in the living room, popping banana bread into her mouth between slurps of tea.

Leaning over my shoulder, Aunt Rhetta slips a steaming fragrant cup between my elbows.

"It's Earl Grey, dear. Make you feel better."

"Did she say when she'd be back?"

"That china pattern is Silver Birch, you know. Got it at a garage sale for fifty cents."

"Aunt Rhetta, did Mother say where she was going or when she'd be back?" I repeat sharply.

Her chin quivers, "No."

"Sorry, I'm not mad at you. Thanks for the tea." It actually does help.

Rhetta sits at the end of the table safely beyond my reach. I force a smile and hope it doesn't look as if I'm baring my teeth.

"Sister," she calls, "come sit with us." Aunt Ida shakes her head and plants her feet further apart. She leans over her lap to reach for more food. "Sister," calls Rhetta, "bring your cup. I've made a fresh pot. Come along now."

Aunt Ida slippers to the table, teacup in one hand, radio in the other. She carries the banana bread in her mouth like an Labrador Retriever.

"What are they talking about this morning, Auntie?" I indicate her earpiece.

"Runaways."

Aunt Rhetta puts the teapot down with more force than necessary. "Your mother IS coming back, dear," she soothes, patting the top of my head.

I feel very young.

Rhetta lowers herself onto a chair and her bones clunk on the wood. As she passes the plate of buttered cake, her face brightens. "Do you remember ... let's see — what would he be to you? Your poor father's sister's son?"

"Cousin Dick?"

"Yes, that's it. Your cousin, Richard."

"I haven't heard about him for years." I pour myself a little more tea. Aunt Rhetta hasn't touched hers yet. "What's he up to?"

"You remember that his mother, your Aunt Jen, had the toy shop?"

"Yeah, it was called ... a funny name."

"Play-With-Me-Jenny," volunteered Rhetta.

"Right! I remember going in there with Richard. He wouldn't let me touch anything. Very bossy."

"Did you know when his mother passed on she left him the shop?"

Aunt Ida pulls the grey plug from her ear and wraps the cord around the radio, pushing it into her pocket. "He was no businessman," she states, "Jenny should'a known that."

"He'd been in business for years, Ida. How can you say that?"

"Having a paper route is not running a business."

"Well, I think it is. You have customers, handle money, etcetera. 'Course it's a business," she defends.

"Why do you stick up for the miserable little shit? He's

56

HIS side of the family, not ours. Riffraff."

"Sister!" Rhetta looks alarmed.

"Don't you sister me." She shakes her stubby finger in Rhetta's direction. "You know very well what he did to the shop."

"What did he do?" I ask tentatively.

"Ruint it. That's what," says Ida over beefy folded arms.

"It went into a decline is all," Rhetta offers.

"It declined right into bankruptcy."

"Be that as it may, Ida. He tried hard, Richard did. He tried real hard," Rhetta emphasizes, hoping to convince me of this.

"Should never have changed the name, bloody fool," adds Ida.

"What does a name change have to do with it?"

Rhetta opens her mouth to reply but instead Ida speaks. "I'll tell her. Then it's done right." She paces the room in measured steps. "Richard had a very big ego," she begins. "He wanted to change the name of the store right away to show his new ownership."

"That's understandable," I encourage. Rhetta smiles agreeably.

"D'ya mind? I'm not through yet," Ida Ruth rebukes, circling the table like a shark around ripe bait.

"He called it … Play-With-Me-Dick. Couldn't understand why business fell off."

"As far as we know, he's running a successful car wash now. In Saskatoon," Rhetta conveys proudly. "Look him up on your travels. You and your mother could pop in there for a wash and wax." She covers her mouth with two fingers. "Sorry, sweets. I didn't mean to remind you."

"It's okay. She'll be walking through that door wanting another meal any minute now." *Yeah, right. And Cousin Dickie will make the Forbes' 100 list.*

I feign a casual saunter to the door to check the road in front. Fine dust rises from the curtain material as I pull it back. Outside, a battered yellow station wagon coughs up to the mailbox. A horn beeps.

"Someone's out here at your mailbox," I call toward the dining room. "Yellow car." They both come at a trot. I stand aside, having seen those elbows in action.

"Mail lady," says Rhetta as she passes.

They jockey on the porch waiting for her to gather the mail from the back of the vehicle. She slams the car door then mounts the walk to the front stairs, pausing at the bottom before labouring up. She climbs like a child, one foot up, then hoists the other to join it. The "other" isn't a foot at all but a peg. She taps her way across the verandah as I watch in fascination. The wooden leg is painted the same colour as her car. She notices my rudeness.

"Lookin' at the peg, are ya?" She lifts the peak of her John Deere cap. "Loggin' accident. Used to be a whistle punk up north."

"Sorry. Didn't mean to stare."

She shrugs it off. "Mornin' ladies. Fine day. Bit of mail here for ya." She reads a parcel in shocking pink wrap. "Says Mizz Ida Basher and it's from …"

"I know where it's from," Ida interrupts, snatching it from the woman's hand.

The rest of the mail falls from under the mail lady's arm and skitters over the porch. I gather and return them to her nicotine-stained fingers.

"Thank ya. Dropping ever'thin' today. Had the jitters since I was almost gunned down by a motorhome."

Couldn't be.

Ida re-enters the house, parcel pressed to her bosom, and kicks shut the door.

"Sister's being secretive, isn't she?" Rhetta directs her attention to the mail lady. "Where's the box from?" she asks slyly.

"Post Office says I can't tell ya. I have to take an oath you know, and sign stuff." The mail lady slides her glasses up her nose.

"Couldn't read it, huh?" asks Rhetta. "Thought you knew everything, Gert. Missing things in your old age?"

"Frederick's of Hollywood," the courier confesses, rising

to the challenge. She turns on her wooden peg leaving a smooth polished circle on the decking.

Rhetta elbows me in the ribs and winks. "Let's go see what Sister's got to say for herself, shall we, sweets?"

Before I go in, I cast an anxious look down Quail's Run Lane for an approaching motorhome. The mail lady does also.

▲

By noon with my things packed and in the car, I say good-bye to the Aunts. "Thank you both for putting us up. It was great fun seeing you again."

"Don't look so sad, sweets. Dixie's a big girl and knows what she's doing." I bend down so Rhetta can fling her arms around my neck. Her elbow joints grate as her hands pat my back. "I'll come to Manitoba with you if you want," she whispers into my ear. "I'd like to see Queenie again and what's-his-name, the barber."

"Albert Fong? No, Auntie, but thanks for the offer. This trip was for Mother's benefit. I'm not going to Manitoba now. No need." I try to straighten but she comes with me. "Everything of hers is upstairs but her make-up bag. She can do her own packing when she gets back." Rhetta's thin arms slide from my shoulders.

"How will your poor mother get home?" Auntie asks, downcast.

"Greyhound. Motorhome. Thumb. Lots of options."

"Can I have her dried flowers if she DOESN'T come back?" asks Rhetta, seeing a new light on the circumstances. "And maybe her goldfish earrings and the golf clubs?"

"Sure, help yourself to anything you want. I'll even bring in the kindling."

With the stone's removal from behind the rear wheel, I'm ready to return home. All that room in the back now. As I turn the ignition key, the radio crackles on and darned if it isn't the tail end of Willie singing 'On the Road Again'. How prophetic. Easing out the clutch, I pull a U-turn and wave at an empty porch. They're already dividing the spoils.

I remember reading of a lovely ceremony in Tibet where the body of the deceased is cut up and the pieces laid out on a large flat rock. Politely waiting vultures sit in an orderly convention overlooking the ritual. It's part of the ceremony that they must wait until invited to eat the remains. When the birds pick the bones clean the bones are thrown into the jungle below the funeral rock. I feel that the meaty part of me is now gone. Nothing left but to throw the bones.

As I return to the Calgary city limits, rain freckles the dusty windshield. I drive past the sign promising that if I follow the road I'll eventually get back to Vancouver. Verna will be very surprised when I walk in without HER mother.

The rain now sluices down as it can only do in Calgary. Smacking the windows. Wanting in. The wipers can't keep up with the volume. I expect at any time to come upon the *Maid of the Mist* bobbing her way through the wet. Traffic has ceased to move beyond a snail's pace. Through the windshield, I see woolly spots of orange light probably indicating the parking lot of a shopping mall. I signal a turn and remove myself from the highway. The hole I leave in the traffic fills in. Parking beneath a lamp standard, I wipe the foggy windows and watch the water course down the glass. It's soothing being warm and secure with the rain above your head. I rub my neck, feeling the tension ease. In the glove compartment I find sesame seed snaps welded together and a deformed Caramilk. Comfort food.

I don't remember falling asleep but I must have because the rain has calmed to a fine drizzle, and it looks as though the sun will burn through. I check my face in the rear-view mirror and brush melted chocolate from my chin. I'd better get at it or I'll be driving directly into the sunset.

The car purrs along the puddled highway and I enjoy a little time for myself. I'll write a book in my head — put it all down on paper when I get back home. A Canadian bestseller. About a little red-haired orphan in PEI. About a prairie farm hand and a kid. All the good stuff is taken. How about a daughter who leaves her mother in the hands of a frenzied, frothing-at-the-mouth sexual pervert? Or "prevert" as Verna would say. He has her bound and gagged. Oh, I like it already. She's wearing skin-tight blue jeans and four-inch rhinestone-studded stiletto heels. He forces her to wear them. Dirty degenerate. He's passing Roquefort cheese beneath her nose and leering. She struggles with her bonds to no avail. He rips her bodice exposing ... no he doesn't. He gambols before her in a fromage cotillion, his hairless white backside gyrating to the erotic beat of Heavy Metal. The Big Cheese threatens to ride again. No, he won't, not on MY mother.

BLEEET!

Her bonds loosen. A knife within her reach ...

BLEEET!!

Go round, for chrissake, can't you see I'm writing? Scarlet-tipped fingers circle the ebony handle ...

BLEEEET!! BLEEET!!

"Yooo Hoooo, Edith." Mother hangs out the window of the motorhome as it draws alongside. "Hi, sweetheart."

I floor the gas pedal, lurching forward. They keep pace, then pull ahead. As they pass, Mother smiles, tips her head slightly, and sweeps the back of her hand at me, fingers slightly curved, waving gently like the Queen Mum journeying to a garden party. They signal and turn onto a side road that looks like it weaves into the foothills. For just an instant, I delight in the idea of roaring away, leaving them behind. But I slow, then follow them. Walter drives cautiously down the road and stops. I do the same, allowing a good hundred feet between us, then lock the doors.

Mother steps heedlessly from the motorhome into the ooze of the country road. Her arms flail searching for balance as her feet slide into the tire ruts. The nearer she gets to the car, the more clay-like gumbo adheres to her shoes making them appear as big as the box they came in. She is inches taller.

If I were a smoker, this would be the time for a cigarette. I could light it dramatically while she waits, then blow the smoke at her as she sticks her face in the car.

"Roll down the window, Edie-pie, so we can have a talk," she coos.

I turn on the radio. Static is better than what is about to come.

"Edith," she raps on the window, "you're just being sulky. I'm the one who should be mad. My shoes are ruined and it's all your fault."

I turn up the radio but it fizzles and dies so I hum loudly.

His nibs, the Munchkin from Yahk, appears in the motorhome's doorway. He daintily extends pointed toes toward the three stairs separating him from Alberta soil. He brushes at his pastel pants accordioned at the crotch, then waits on the bottom step.

"She won't speak to me, Walter," Mother yells in her best fishmonger voice. "Walter!" She motions him on. "You talk to her."

"Give it up," I warn.

Walter re-enters the motorhome, starts it up, then backs it closer to my front bumper. When he emerges, a plastic garbage bag covers each foot. He holds onto the tops as he tip-toes halfway to my car through the mire.

"Edith," he calls, "your mother and I are sorry for any

bother we may have caused you." He looks into his garbage bags then pleats the plastic back into his fists. "We lost track of time. Come sit with us in the mo …"

"… motorhome," finishes Mother, patting his arm.

"… motorhome, and have a coffee."

I unlock the car door and grudgingly get out. "Your behaviour is really pissing me off," I whisper low enough so Walter won't hear.

"My behaviour? What about yours? At least I have a perfectly good explanation," says Mother brightly.

"You always do."

She sets her jaw, glaring. "Just what does that mean?"

"You always come up with some *perfectly good* explanation for screwing up my life."

She looks as if she's just been goosed. Walter minces his way back to the motorhome. A judicious retreat.

"How can you say that?"

"Easy."

"I've always wanted what's best for you girls."

"See? See? You girls!" I yell. "We're not talking 'you girls' here. We're talking, ME, for a change. ME, understand?"

A square-wheel of thunder clatters across the low cloud ceiling. Water plops into the wet earth.

"Were you thinking about ME when you up and buggered off this morning? Not bloody likely. It's always been YOU first, then Verna, then Dad, then a toss-up between me and whatever dog we had roaming around."

Rain quivers on her earlobe like an exquisite diamond as she spikes out her answer. "Bullshit!" The drop falls. Walter's stereo plays "Swan Lake" on all six speakers. He slides open a window near the back of the motorhome and increases the volume.

"What about my grade seven graduation, huh?"

"How far back are we going here, Edith?"

We circle each other, slogging our way through the muck while Walter's swans touch wings and step delicately through their dance *en pointe*.

"I could go farther back but at your age time is precious."

"O-h-h-h, it's cut and slash, is it?"

"Yeah, nothing like a little bloodletting." I give her a gallows smile and lean against the car. "Can you even remember who I went with?"

"Of course. It was Luisa Vespucci's boy. The oldest one. Gerald." Mother looks as pleased now as when Gerald unexpectedly arrived on our doorstep dressed in his hand-me-down brown suit.

Gerald was a great oaf who smelled funny, like food about to go bad. I'd told him I'd meet him by the goalposts at school but he shows up at the house anyway with his freshly squeezed zits and his lip hung up on his braces.

"You think I wanted to go with Gerald?"

"You were the one moaning about not having anyone to go with. After you'd bought that dress and all."

"I didn't buy that dress," I argue. "YOU did."

"You're outta your mind. You loved that dress. Just HAD to have it. All that pink ribbon and net."

"Didn't even want to go. Graduation was no big deal."

"You don't remember flinging yourself around the house because everyone in the world had a date but you. Luisa had said at the last bridge game that her Gerald, popular as he was, didn't have one either."

"Understandable." *I'm positive SHE got that dress.* "You made me go," I insist.

"Me? Make you do something you didn't want to do?" she asks caustically, hands on hip. "Since when?"

"You blackmailed me into going with that lard-assed little creep," I charge.

"He wasn't that bad," she champions.

"Believe me, he was. When I say lard-assed I know what I'm talking about."

"Did you … ?"

"Did I what? Have s-e-x?"

"I don't want to know," she says, covering her ears.

I bang the hubcap with my heel, dislodging a lump of mud from under the fender. Walter mistakes the lapse in our animated discussion for a cease-fire and lowers the music.

"Oh, Mother, you're gonna know!" I promise. "That lumbering hulk Gerald walked me home from the dance. I said I could do it myself but Gerald said, 'Your mother told us to have a good time.' You listening, Mother? Then he pinned me to a tree and dropped his pants. It happened so fast, I think he'd been undoing them all along."

Mother lowers her hands from her ears and measures a few steps in either direction before returning my look.

"Then what?" she asks, hugging her arms across her stomach.

"I kneed him in the balls." I repeat the action of that June night.

She slaps both hands over her mouth and wheels around, her back to me. She sucks air between her teeth as if I'd kicked *her*.

"Bone on bone," I elaborate, enjoying the moment. "When he pitched forward his braces caught on my dress. Took out half a yard of pink net. Last I saw he was on his hands and knees — his bare bum shining in the ferns."

"So-o-o, that's why Luisa dropped me from the bridge club." She lifts her head at the sudden insight.

"So-o-o, we're back to you again. 'Gee, Edith, sweetheart,' I mock, 'I'm so-o-o sorry. It was all MY fault for interfering.'"

"My fault, hell! How was I to know?" Mother swipes at the water trickling down her neck. "But when it came to not going or going with Gerald, the decision was yours."

"Crap," I mumble. *She can't be right. I'd remember a thing like that.* I sit on one end of the bumper and hang over my outstretched legs watching the water weep onto the sodden ground ... *Wouldn't I?* "How about the time," I say, drawing in my legs, "you wouldn't let me go out with Benny Sawyer?"

She frowns, "Who?"

"Benny Sawyer. Grade Ten. He was in my math class."

She shakes her head.

"That was SO monumental — and you don't remember."

I stab my finger toward the end of her nose. "Benny was only THE most gorgeous, most popular, smartest guy in the class. He always came to school in a suit and tie, then he'd drive home, changing clothes again at noon." When I drift off recalling how elegant he was in that petrie dish of low-life intelligence, she brings me back.

"And ... ?"

"You MUST remember," I insist. "I told you at supper Benny and I were going out?" I stop long enough to see if there's any reaction, then continue. "When he came to pick me up that night you sent me to my room, then met him at the door yourself and told him I had a headache and wouldn't be going."

"Ahh," she says, her eyes brightening. "Him."

"Him!"

"Your father said he was a gangster."

"So?"

"Well, Toots, having a daughter go out with a criminal wasn't covered in Dr. Spock."

"You didn't trust me. That's what it was." I had watched through the crack in my bedroom door. He had looked so beautiful leaning against the doorjamb. Behind him, the polish on his new car paled in comparison.

"You could have told him yourself."

"At sixteen I'm supposed to tell him my mother won't let me out?"

She arches her eyebrows in answer.

Benny had nodded knowingly next day and gave me a pitying smile. He reigned as king until the end of school year, then headed for the big city.

"All I wanted was one date." I place my hands on her shoulders. "ONE!"

"Water under the bridge," she states, squirming away.

"Swan Lake" trembles from the motorhome as Odette begins fluttering her last.

Mother slogs half a dozen paces before turning. "Edith?"

"Wha'?" I'm so tired.

"Are you through knocking me?"

"Hell, no."

"You've got less than two minutes," she warns, tapping her watch.

66

I launch right in even though two minutes won't make a dint. "You opened my mail ..."

"Maybe. But only when it got too close to the kettle."

I hold up my hand like a traffic cop signalling her to stop. "You listened in on phone calls, checked to see if I was really baby-sitting alone, rummaged through my dresser drawers looking for God-knows-what ..."

"Just making sure you were staying out of trouble. Teenage girls are a worry, and I had a double dose."

"What about trust?"

"I had a job to do," she responds angrily, stomping toward the motorhome.

"As warden?"

She turns again, fists jammed into her hips. "Raising you girls on your father's salary wasn't easy." Two flash points bloom on her cheekbones. "Sometimes there were no commissions. Sometimes he spent half of it before he even got home."

"That didn't give you the right to target me with YOUR insecurities." From the highway a sound of sudden braking and the reprimanding horn of a transport truck.

"We're alike, Edith, you and I."

"Oh, pull-ee-e-z-e."

"You looked out for Verna, didn't you?"

"Well, she was younger."

"Uh huh."

"I never went looking in her diary."

"I did," she says, banging on the door of the motorhome.

"Is nothing sacred?"

She hauls open Walter's door to call inside. "Can we get a couple of towels, Walter?" She leans on her elbow while he fetches. "Gotta get in there and kill those freakin' swans."

"If you want to ride with him," I jerk my thumb past her nose, "instead of me, just say so. I'll be more than happy to go home. My holidays, my car, and I'm calling the shots."

"Of course, dear," she says with a sincerity that raises the hair on the back of my neck. She thanks Walter, then mops at her face, speaking into the towel.

"What did you just say?" I question.

She wraps the towel around her hair before responding. "I said, I guess I'll ride with you."

"Then let's go."

"Does this mean I'm still in the running for Mother of the Year?"

"Not a hope in hell."

Walter has positioned himself at the top of the stairs with additional towels, more to save his vehicle than from hospitality, I suppose.

"What a guy," she says warmly.

"Come in, girls, now you've had your little chat."

"We're leaving," I tell him. *Please, no fanfares, no twenty-one gun salutes.* "Got to make up for lost time."

"Speaking of 'making up', Edith, gimme a minute to say goodbye to my sweetie?"

I sigh dramatically. "I'll start the car."

"But I've made coffee," he fusses, sweeping his arms like a *maitre d'* indicating our table. Mother follows him up, removing her shoes at his gentle suggestion.

"Mother!"

She doesn't even turn around to see my reaction as she pulls my car keys from her sleeve and jingles them tauntingly over her shoulder.

I wonder if lying right here and banging my heels on the floor would make me feel better? "Half a cup." I feel as though I have surrendered to the foe. "Half a cup, d'ya hear me?"

Walter looks nervous until I remove my shoes and flip them on top of the muddy garbage bags. He supplies Mother with a robe and me with a towel. She goes off to find a bathroom.

"Want a sweater?" asks Walter tipping onto his toes.

I decline. I'm tough, I can take being a little spongy. I try not to be impressed with the interior of this place. Flowers everywhere; in the sink, on the microwave, the easy chairs, everywhere.

He invites me to the table. "Plastic," he assures, stroking the padded bench seat.

I push aside more blooms to sit at a most unusual table. It's like gazing into a tidal pool. Within the depths of the turquoise fibreglass are coloured shells, pink starfish in rigid perfection and amputated fingers of coral. "Oh, my gaw-w-wd!" So much for indifference.

"It's beautiful, isn't it?" says Mum emerging in her terrycloth cocoon. "See the little school of seahorses? Cute, eh? Walter had it made specially."

"Yeah, it's ... um ... different." I wonder if there's an admission charge.

"Coffee, Edith? You girls must be cold. Maybe we could have the croissants now?"

Mother opens the fridge, pulling out a white bakery box, then hip-checks the door closed. *She is entirely too at home here.* "I'll put 'em in the oven. We'll have them with Walter's homemade jelly." From a cupboard above her head she takes a jar and sets it on the counter. Placed over the oceanic tableau are three lacy placemats. Walter crochets, too?

"Want to throw your clothes in the dryer?" she asks over the coffeepot. "No? Well, suit yourself."

I pointedly indicate half a cup and she pointedly ignores me, setting full mugs before us. Walter's rolled shirt sleeves expose wrists as blue-veined as some of the riper cheese he sells.

"Thank you," I say tightly.

Mother sits opposite, next to Walter. "What I tried to tell you, Edith — before our little talk — Walter came by the Aunts' early this morning when you were still sleeping. There I was sitting on the front porch watching the clouds and he drove up. He invited me along to pick flowers." *And just how did he know you were there?* "His son has a ranch here, you know. Imagine, wildflowers, just ready for the taking."

I imagine SHE was too, after a romp in the grass with Walter. I try the coffee. It's good and strong.

"Anyway," she continues, "after meeting Walter's son — you'll like him, dear — we went picking." She indicates the result with a roll of her arm.

"Did you really expect to get all these into the trunk of the Mercedes?"

She looks surprised. "It never crossed my mind because we were having such a lovely time." She smiles at Walter, who dips his head shyly.

"We tried phoning," he says, "but the cell was down. Probably the rain."

"Cell?" I ask, Luddite that I am.

"Cell phone," says Mother, now on her way to the oven. "Walter has one up front between the seats."

"Of course he does."

"We were in a valley out of range," he adds.

"I understand why you were late. I'm not happy about it, but I understand," I say magnanimously.

Mother pats the top of my head, then puts the pan of warm croissants in front of us.

"Hot. Hot." Walter says excitedly, fluttering his hands. Mother scrambles to fling a protective mat on the table. Walter checks for surface damage before gliding it beneath the croissants.

"How did you find me on the highway? The Aunts?"

"We drove in not long after you left," Mother answers. "The Aunts were anxious that we catch you so Walter drove hell-bent-for-election down the highway." She slides in close to him. "But it was raining so hard we couldn't see. We turned back and by that time it had cleared."

"Dixie saw you," Walter says proudly, dabbing at her damp hair with his napkin.

"You didn't see US, Edith, on the other side of the highway?" Mother nuzzles his hand. "No, you would have stopped, wouldn't you, dear?"

I bite my tongue.

"I'll need some dry clothes from the car," she states.

"Good luck."

"What's that supposed to mean."

"I don't have your clothes."

It takes a moment for this to sink in. "Didn't you pack them?"

Walter squirms uncomfortably as I make wet coffee rings on his table, linking the circles before answering. "Nope."

"And why not?"

"I wasn't privy to your plans."

"Privy to my plans?" she echoes.

Walter's head swivels like an observer at a tennis match.

"I didn't know whether you were even coming back."

She blinks twice.

"I left your stuff as I found it, hung up on the floor."

"Wha-a-a-t?" she brays.

I snicker. "The Aunts didn't tell you?"

She collapses against the back of the seat. "Not a word."

"You can kiss your stuff goodbye, then. Those two will be decked out arguing over who got the best sweater."

"I'll kill those old bid ..." she sputters.

Walter's eyebrows collide over his nose.

"Water under the bridge, eh Mum?"

She turns to Walter with a forced smile. "Hey, they're welcome to them," she says, nibbling the tip from her croissant. "Time for a change anyway. Think I'll start a whole new life. New friends," she looks through her lashes at Walter, "new clothes. A new me."

As she wasn't looking for confirmation, I didn't give any.

"My son has invited us to dinner. We'd like you to come, Edith. Will you?" Walter manages to address me without making eye contact. His vision wavers about ear level.

"We gotta go. Manitoba's not getting any closer."

"Walter has to go back to work tomorrow and this will be our last chance for a visit," says Mother, affecting a little pout.

Finally rid of him! "In that case I guess we can spare a few hours. Sure, Walter. Dinner."

Mum smiles confidently over the rim of her cup. Damn, she's unnerving.

With the pseudo-pleasantries out of the way, and her newly-dried clothes on, I escort her from the motorhome. The rain has eased. Mother calls back to tell Walter we'll be right behind.

He turns the Winnebago in a large circle on the grassy field and retraces his way over the ruts in the road. I do likewise, hearing the gumbo hitting the underside of the car as the wheels spin beneath us.

"This friggin' radio's broken again," I say sourly, dropping all pretense of politeness, "and this better be the goddam finale of your romantic encounter with the Cheese Man."

"One more dinner," she says, applying an excess of Luscious Plum to her lips. She screws down the top before adding, "but we intend to get together in Vancouver."

"I DON'T CARE ABOUT VANCOUVER. I just want to get this trip over with. I still don't know how I got talked into it. You'd have been better off flying."

"I am flying, Toots," she chuckles, resisting my effort to be as vile as possible, "and Snuggy-buns is the reason."

"Quaint. Got any Gravol?"

"What's sticking in your craw?" She snaps her purse shut. "Why don't you like him? Huh? Huh?"

"He's a pickup. You don't even know him ..."

"I know him," she says stubbornly.

"Let me finish. You're a little old for all this coquettishness. As for screwing him ..."

She slugs me. As hard as she can, she punches my arm. The car veers to the right before I straighten the wheel.

"Hey! I'm driving. Do you mind?"

"Edith, you're a miserable, hateful, up-tight woman, who probably hasn't had a night of passion in your whole life — other than Gerald," she adds maliciously.

I stiffen. "That wasn't passion."

"Mine is, so just back off and let me have it."

I'll let her have it, alright. The silence in the car is deafening. I smack the radio with the heel of my hand. Nothing.

Three miles down the road Mother is almost apologizing. "I still think you're unhappy — but not hateful." She points ahead. "Walter's changing lanes."

"I can see, damn it."

Mother chooses to ignore my brittle mood and instead

72

whistles a march tune, keeping time with her mud-stained shoes. I believe she's been trained in psychological warfare. An honours student. I continue with the vendetta she started. "I may be unhappy but I'm happy being that way. It's me."

"Did you hear what you just said?" she snorts. "You're happy being unhappy."

"Yeah, yeah." I give up the one-sided battle, saving my ammunition for a later skirmish. "How far is this place? The son's house?"

"Just follow. We'll get there." She faces me, twisting as far as she can in her seatbelt. "I should warn ... um, tell you about Maurice."

"Maurice? Walter's son is a Mo-r-r-e-e-ece? Mo for short?"

"How do you know?"

"Am I right? Mo for SHORT. Get it?"

"He's taller than Walter."

"A gopher on its hind legs is taller than Walter."

"I choose to ignore that." She sucks her tooth. "Do you want to know about Maurice, or not?"

"Not. Tell me instead about Mrs. Mo and all the little Muckles."

"There aren't any."

"Gee, no little Muckles. Too bad." Walter's flasher light is blinking before me.

"No Mrs. Mo either. He's turning left, Edith."

"I KNOW, I can see." I follow, crossing the highway. "This guy is single? Is this a set-up? You wouldn't be pulling a Gerald again, would you, Mother?"

"Hackles down. He's, uhh, not your type but it certainly wouldn't hurt to be nice." She checks her face in the mirror. "Maurice is ... different. Here's the house. Just pull in behind Walter."

"Different how?" I am beginning to grasp the obvious.

The driveway circles before a split-level house set in well-tended gardens. Beyond, a traditional white trimmed red barn throws a shadow over squat wooden outbuildings. With livestock dotting the fields it makes a picturesque scene.

From the doorway a woman in a long-sleeved white scoop-neck blouse and black skirt waves a welcome.

"Oh great. Nobody mentioned dressing for dinner. I'm a mess, and look at her." I point toward the house. "She's dressed to the nines."

The woman picks up her long skirt to step over the doorway. She walks carefully in her heels to the railing of the verandah. Leaning over, her blond hair sweeps her face. She reaches up to remove a comb then re-pins the hair in place.

"I feel pretty shabby. Do you think I should change?"

Mother just shakes her head no, and opens the car door. I grab her before she slides out. "I thought you said there was no Mrs. Muckle."

"There isn't."

Hedonism must run in the family. I take my time kicking the rock behind the rear tire, letting Walter go ahead. Mother waits for me at the bottom of the stairs while I try to rasp the gumbo off my shoes by rubbing them together. She pinches my arm when no one's looking.

"Oww. What the hell is that for?" I whisper, massaging the spot.

"You'll see." She crosses before me and lightly mounts the stairs. I lumber behind her, head down. All three wait for me at the top.

"Edith, I'd like you to meet Maurice, my son."

"Dad!" she admonishes, placing a hand on his chest.

"Oh, sorry. Edith, I'd like you to meet Maxine, my son."

Beneath the luxurious hair is an expertly made-up face, and cheeks that are beginning to show a five-o'clock shadow.

I don't know where to look. I really don't see her outstretched hand, the perfectly groomed outstretched hand until Mother nudges me. I grasp the hand. It returns a firm grip.

"Very nice to meet you, Edith," she says in a pleasant low voice. "Your mother was telling me about you this morning at breakfast."

"Pleased to meet you, uhhh Maxine."

"Come on in, dinner's almost ready. I've got cold drinks waiting." She turns, lifting her skirt to enter the house.

I shoot Mother a look, but she is smiling at Walter. He pats her on the bum and she skips ahead, following Maxine. I remain on the porch trying to absorb the preceding events but Walter bobs back to the doorway, holding open the screen.

"Come on," he urges, "the flies are getting in."

A pitcher of lemonade sweats on the low coffee table in the living room. This is not the parlour of two old Aunts. It's done in frosted green and dusty rose. Watercolours of the prairie landscape are tastefully displayed against the shot silk walls. Fresh flowers withstand the heat in long crystal vases. *I bet she even cuts the stems underwater like you're supposed to.*

I clutch my glass and press into the corner of the leather chair conscious of the drying mud on my runners, the laces missing the little tips.

"So, Edith," says Maxine, crossing her legs, "Your mother says you're a writer."

"Yes."

"What do you write?" She leans toward me with interest, well-shaped eyebrows arched.

"Copy for the Sears catalogue."

"Oh." She sits back, eyes losing their lustre.

"But I am working on a novel," I add creatively.

"Do tell." She sips from her glass, leaving a glossy pink imprint on the rim. "What's it about?"

"It's about a murder ... a murderer who ... um, kills an interfering mother ... HER mother."

"It doesn't sound as though you're too far into the story," Maxine editorializes.

"Oh, yes, I'm more than halfway. We writers don't care to reveal plots. We're a bit murky on details. You know how it is."

"I do indeed, dear heart," she says, graciously ignoring my condescending attitude. "I'm a writer, too."

Isn't everybody? "What are you attempting?"

"I've just completed the final book in a trilogy. Before that I published, oh, about a dozen or so novels."

"Oh." *Good one, Edith. Caught with your foot firmly lodged in your mouth.*

Maxine continues, "I write Romance novels. I know, don't tell me," she holds up her hand. "Real writers such as yourself don't consider Romance writers as authors of any substance, but it does pay the bills."

"A published writer, imagine," gushes Mother. "I'd love to read one of your books, Maxine."

"I have some in the library. I can't resist a fan's request." She sweeps from the room.

I try to catch Mother's eye. She snuggles up to Walter when he drops his arm around her shoulders. "What time are you leaving tomorrow?" she asks him.

"After breakfast, honey. No big rush. Soon as I see you girls on the road I'll head out."

"Mum and I are leaving right after dinner, Walter, NOT breakfast." Somebody got their wires crossed. "Got a lot of ground to cover tonight."

"Did you hear that, Maurice?" Walter asks as Maxine re-enters the room with an armful of paperbacks. "These girls want to head out right after dinner. Eat and run, eh?"

"Ladies, puh-le-e-se," Maxine poses gracefully, "I've already made accommodations. There's puh-lenty of room." She sets the books beside Mother. "Dad has his Winnebago and there's a suite in the basement that will be most comfortable. Dixie, you fox, you knew you had an invitation this morning."

Let me at her! Disembowelment with a spoon.

"There, Edith, you see? How can we refuse?" says Mother, buffing Walter's fleshy knee. "I hope it's not an imposition, Maxine."

"No. No. No-o-o. It'll be nice to have some female companionship." With the back of her hand she pushes at her hair. The whole thing shifts. Just a little askew. As she hikes up her skirt to cross her legs, I see black tufts coiling through the patterned stockings. "Edith," Maxine says, "you appear preoccupied with my appearance. Is there something wrong?" She runs her hands over her thighs, smoothing the black material.

Mother is suddenly alert waiting for me to commit a social *faux pas*. I finally have her attention. Eye contact.

"I'm, uhh ... not used to being in the company of ... of ..."

"Prairie women dressing for dinner?" suggests Maxine.

"No, that's not it. It's more like not used to seeing women with uhh ... a five-o'clock shadow."

Mother gasps and pats her chest. Walter looks elsewhere. Maxine starts to smile. Then she laughs. A robust, ribald laugh. The hair slips forward inching toward her eyebrows.

"Never could keep the damn thing on straight. Pardon my French."

"What's underneath?" I ask.

"Nothing." She lifts the wig to expose a suntanned bald head with a fringe of dark hair circling below.

"That's your problem, no grip. I think you can buy suckers or something."

"It's probably worth looking into," she says, replacing the wig and grinding it into place. "I'll check on dinner."

Mother bites her lip, not too sure about what just happened.

"It's ready," calls Maxine from the kitchen. "Come sit up."

I'm the first to stand.

It was a wonderful meal of beef tenderloin, fiery homemade horseradish, fresh vegetables from the garden and bottles of cold plum wine. After the second piece of cheesecake I admit I can eat no more.

"Why don't you show Edith around the farm while there's

still light?" Walter says, removing his toothpick. "Dixie and I will clean up, won't we, Dix?"

"Oh. Oh, sure," says Mum without enthusiasm.

"Back in a jiff, Edith," says the retreating Maxine, "don't want to snag my nylons."

"Nice of you to help with dishes, Mother." I stack my plate with the silverware and push it in her direction. "Something in your eye? You seem to be squinting."

As I finish my coffee, Maxine enters the kitchen in jeans, boots and a flowered shirt. A silk scarf thrown over her hair knots beneath her chin. "That should hold it down while we have our tour." She opens the screen door for me then stands aside.

"Old habits die hard?" I say in passing.

She shrugs. "Guess so," and shuts the screen. A gold and white collie bounds up to greet her, then trots ahead.

"Do you cross-dress all the time?"

"Don't be shy, Edith, speak right up."

"Sorry." I match her stride for stride. "Do you? Farmers are supposed to be rough-and-tumble."

"Firstly, I'm a rancher not a farmer. Secondly, I don't do chores looking like this. I don't even go to town looking like this, although I probably could."

"Nobody knows?"

"My close friends do, of course. Some suspect, but nothing overt has been said. Not to my face anyway. People let me live my life."

"Your father is very accepting."

"He wasn't at first. We had terrible rows. My brother is a bit of an asshole about it, if you must know." We reach the first outbuilding. She slides the door to one side. "This is the nursery for newborns who need feeding or for heifers having their first calf." The building is empty but the stalls have sweet, clean hay on the floor.

"Do you think of yourself as a him or her?"

"Her. It's not calving time so there's no livestock in here now." She closes the door and proceeds through the yard. "This chute is for castrating bull calves." She rubs her hand over the chipped red paint of the metal bars.

"You're not threatened by that, are you?"

"Jesus, Edith, you're like a pitbull," she complains.

"Well, I don't know anybody like you. How am I supposed to be an informed person if I don't ask? You've had years to live with it, I've had a couple of hours."

"What do you want to know?" Maxine says with resignation.

"I don't know what I want to know. When I think of something, can I ask?"

"I suppose," she says.

"Good, now show me the rest."

We follow the dog who trots ahead to investigate a coulee. The Russian olive trees outlined against the flushed evening sky house a senate of starlings arguing points of order. This must be where they came for flowers this morning.

"I think we'd better head back. My mother and your father are alone in that house."

"They can be alone, Edith. They're adults."

"I don't want to encourage her to be a consenting adult." Maxine turns, one hand on her hip. "You don't like my dad?"

"I dunno." I move past.

She taps me on the shoulder. "What do you mean, you don't know?"

"Don't get your shirt in a knot. I don't know him, that's all."

"Why should it matter if you know him or not? Your mother can have her own friends without your approval."

"Listen, Bub, doesn't it bother you that all of a sudden

your father has himself a lady friend? You know nothing about my mother. Or me for that matter."

She counts off on her fingers. "Dad told me your mum's a widow. That your father died of carbon-monoxide poisoning after shutting himself in the garage. That you have a younger sister, Verna ..."

"My father's death was accidental," I break in curtly.

"Hey," she throws up her hands, "I never presumed otherwise."

"He forgot the car was running. He was living with Alzheimer's."

"I'm sorry about that," Maxine says scuffing at the ground. She turns and continues walking, calling over her shoulder, "Anyway, it doesn't matter because whatever Dixie's doing, she's doing right. Dad's a happy man. Hasn't been that way for quite a while. He doesn't like being alone. Nobody does."

"Ahh, shit."

"You don't like that they're happy?"

"No, I mean ahh, shit." I hold up my runner and show her the fresh green cow pie clinging to the leather.

"Serves you right."

When we re-enter the house we see the contented couple sitting on the floor, backs against the sofa. Open across their knees are photo albums.

"Dad, are you dragging out those old school pictures again?"

"Well, son, Dixie wanted to look at them."

"I'll bet it didn't take much persuading, did it, Dix? He's only too happy to show them off."

"I love to look at family histories. Pictures tell so much about a person. All that body English," Mother says.

Body English? She's been reading Cosmo again. "Gee, Mum, you're full of surprises. I didn't know you liked family pictures that much. Don't you keep ours in a cardboard box in the root cellar?"

"Edith's being facetious," she says, flushing, "I don't have a root cellar."

"Where DO you keep the pictures?" I persist.

"Edith, sit down and shut up. I'm having a very nice time here."

I lump myself onto the chesterfield, knotting my arms over my chest. "Sorry," I mumble. "I must learn to hold my tongue while the adults are speaking."

Maxine sits next to me then leans over to stage-whisper, "Bad Edith. Bad, bad Edith." She removes her headscarf and folds it into a neat square, then detaches her wig, placing it on top of her knee. "Want a drink?" The dark fringe of long wispy hair is crimped over her damp scalp. The coral eye shadow expertly applied earlier is now collecting into the creases of her eyelids. One of her dangling earrings is locked into a right angle. "What's so funny?" she inquires.

"You're a mess."

"Well, thanks. I needed that." She/he runs both hands over his head.

"It's okay, Max. Now you look more like me. Rumpled. Used."

He excuses himself and I hear water running in a nearby bathroom. When he returns, he looks more Maurice-like with his face now scrubbed clean of makeup, his hair combed over his head. "Drinks, anyone?" he asks, rubbing his palms together. "I have Grand Marnier or Tia Maria."

We settle down to propose a toast.

"Here's to safe travel," says Walter, clinking glasses with Mother.

"Here's to safe sex," says Maurice, clinking mine.

"Edith! Edith get up." The voice scrapes away the warm fuzzies like claws on a metal door. "I thought you wanted to hit the road at dawn."

Maxine has wonderful down-filled comforters. I hunker into mine, covering my ears from the rude intrusion. "Is it?"

"Is it what?"

"Is it dawn?" I ask, stretching extravagantly.

"No, dear, it's Mother," she says, being cute.

"Just gimme the time."

"The big hand is on the twelve and the little hand is on the nine."

"The big hand is on the twel ..." I swing my legs over the side of the bed, hugging the blanket to my chest. "You mean to tell me it's nine o'clock?"

"Yup."

"I wanted to be out of here early."

"So you said." She slurps her coffee while leaning against the door frame.

"Consider me dressed," I say, reaching for yesterday's clothes. "Did you pack your stuff in the car?"

"I don't have any stuff. The Aunts are wearing it, remember?"

"Borrow something snappy from Maurice."

"I think I'll wait upstairs until you're civil." Halfway up the stairs she calls back, "Maxine has made breakfast but I could toss you down a piece of raw meat if you prefer."

I bunch the comforter against my mouth and scream.

⚓

Beside a vase of fresh chrysanthemums on the kitchen table is a tent of lavender notepaper. The note is written with a fountain pen in a loose spidery black sprawl. Just a sweet old-fashioned girl.

Edith.
Please help yourself to breakfast. I've made a
picnic lunch for you and Dixie to take on the
road. I enjoyed meeting you. Call in on the
way back.
Fondly,
Max

"Did you talk to him?" I ask after reading it.

"Sort of, while I was seeing Walter off."

"Walter's gone, too?"

"'fraid so," she sighs. "He couldn't wait for you. He has calls to make."

I pour a coffee then butter an oversize bran muffin freckled with blueberries. "This is really very nice of Maxine, don't you think?"

"It was just Maurice when he left this morning. The hair didn't go with him," says Mum looking out the window toward the pasture.

"Doesn't matter. He's a nice guy."

"Glad you like him, Edith. Maybe someday he'll be the older sister you never had. My three girls." I open my mouth to protest but she holds up her hand, "Just kidding."

"Better be." I check my watch, then write a thank you on the back of Maxine's paper. We put the dishes in the machine and take a last look around for anything we might have missed, before heading to the car. "Let's go."

"What's the plan for today?" she asks as she buckles herself in.

I delay answering until I wrist-wrestle the Mercedes into first gear. "Lunch at the Hat then straight on to Regina."

"Is Regina before or after Indian Head?"

"Check the map." I offer the new one from the side pocket. "You can let go of it, Edith."

"Make sure you ..."

"I know, I know, fold it along the original lines. You're such a wussie." I wince when she cracks the map over her knee. "Indian Head comes after Regina. Good."

She's so emphatic, a prickling sensation creeps up the back of my neck. *Don't ask*.

"What did you and Walter do after I went to bed?"

"Looked at more pictures of his family ..."

"Speaking of family ..." I broach.

"... and talked about his three wives."

"What three wives?"

"Flowers, all of them. Iris, Daisy and Marigold."

"Sounds like a dairy herd. Where are they?"

"Dead," she says bluntly.

"All of them?"

"Yup, all of them."

"Damn good thing we left. You might have been next."

"Edith! It was very sad. He said Iris had galloping consumption. Daisy died when she fell off the roof. She was fixing shingles," she hastily adds after catching my look. "Or was it Iris fell off the roof? Anyway, Marigold drowned in a flash flood in Spain when her horse threw her into a river. That was a couple of years after she abandoned Walter and her boys."

"That's awful. Maurice did mention a brother."

"They're very close — the boys," Mum emphasises, crossing her fingers to show just how close. "Maurice and Mantovanni and their dad."

"Their mother had a thing for Ms."

"Walter knew Marigold was wrong for him from the beginning because she pined for musicians. He met her at a dance. He happened to be holding a friend's saxophone when she threw herself at his feet. He didn't tell her it wasn't his."

"So she married him for his instrument?" She looks at me to see if I'm being facetious. I hide it well.

"Apparently. He says he can play a paper and comb but it didn't have the same appeal."

"That's understandable. So, two kids later she fled?"

"Yeah. She named the boys after musicians as a constant reminder of what he wasn't."

"Who is Maurice named after?"

"Ravel. You know, Bolero? Mantovanni is self-explanatory."

"Eclectic tastes. So, where is Manto ...?"

"They call him Vonnie. Oh, he's nearby."

"Is he another Maurice/Maxine?"

"Quite the opposite. You'll like him."

"On the contrary, Mother. I can't like anybody I won't meet."

She reaches into her purse and digs around the contents. "Gum?" An unwrapped stick is shoved into my mouth.

"How log has dis been in your bag?"

"Not long. Bought it when I went to Seattle with the Garden Club." I notice she doesn't take one herself.

"Dat was las year," I say around the obstacle. I finally pitch it out the open window. "Jeez, it's like chewing on a tongue depressor."

"You're always complaining."

As Mother dozes, her sunglasses reflect our sail through the prairie ocean. The wind eddies, and the grasses shimmer in the warm afternoon. The odd bird surveys the landscape from a fencepost.

Finally she wakes, looking like she's going to yawn but from her gaping mouth an unexpected song spills.

"... waving wheat, it sure smells sweet when the wind comes right behind the ra-a-ain." She sits upright to sing the rest, throwing out her arms. "O-O-O-Ok-lahoma-a ... O, K, H, A, L, A, no — O, K, L, H, A ... YEOWWW!"

"I think you just spelled Oakalla."

"Whatever." She stretches and looks around. "So, where are we?"

"We just passed Kansas. Look, there's Toto."

"Droll, Edith, very droll."

"We hit Medicine Hat about ten minutes before you burst into song."

"Can we eat soon? I'm starving."

"I know. All your tummy rumbling made me think the poor old car was giving up the ghost. We'll have Maxine's lunch?"

"May as well. It's in the trunk."

"Watch for a side road off the highway."

Mother slides her sunglasses to the end of her nose and peers intently over the top. "Trees ahead."

I signal left even though there's no car closely following. The Mercedes crunches the gravel of the lane Mother pointed out, then glides to a tentative stop on a shady slope. Once outside, I kick the rock into place behind the tire. "Good eye, Mum, this is perfect. You stretch your legs and I'll get lunch."

From the back seat she retrieves her pillow and pitches it at the bottom of a poplar tree.

"This is quite the elegant basket." I carry it to where Mother is sitting, legs straight out, ankles crossed.

Inside the wicker container is a folded red-and-white checkered cloth. I open it, spreading it between us.

"Will you look at this?" I say, placing the basket in the middle. "French bread, two cheeses, paté," I hold them up in turn. "Here's a tub of cream to go with the bananas." Inside the lid, held in place by sturdy bands of elastic, are two china plates. Red linen napkins enfold spoons and little spreading knives with fruit-like handles. I undo a bottle nestled along the side. "Rhubarb wine. Homemade rhubarb wine. It's still cold. Look, Max has even put in wine glasses." I ping the sides. "Real crystal."

"We should issue him a sainthood," says Mum, smoothing the napkin over her lap.

We raise high our glasses and salute Saint Max of the Foothills.

Around a hunk of bread mounded with herb paté I comment, "Pretty sneaky of him, really. This means we have to call in on the way back to return this stuff."

Mother finishes the drink and tips her glass higher to catch the last drops on her tongue. As she reaches for more, she says, "Looks like a message there, Edith. What's it say?"

I hadn't noticed, but folded into one of the elastics is a piece of familiar lavender paper with the same black scrawl.

> *Enjoy!*
> *You hold in your hand glasses that were once lifted to the lips of Russian aristocracy — the Romanovs. Just leave everything with Vonnie so it's not in your way. Dixie has directions.*
> *Fondly,*
> *MAX*

"Imagine, Edith. Antique wine glasses."

"What's he mean, 'Dixie has directions'?"

"It's self-explanatory. We drop the basket at Vonnie's."

"Now where would that be?" I ask warily.

"Umm, past Regina. More wine?"

"Mother, Newfoundland is 'past Regina'. Where does this Vonnie live, exactly?"

"Indian Head."

"Ha! I knew it." In my haste to scramble to my feet I spill my wine. "Dammit, you're doing it again, aren't you?"

"I have no idea what you're babbling on about." She uprights my glass. "And if you're going to spill the stuff, you're not getting any more."

"Listen, you. We were going to drive straight to Manitoba. Period. We're three days on the road and still haven't got out of Alberta. Why is that, Mother?"

"Edith. Sit down and shut up!"

"Stuff it. You're back to running my life. It's not going to happen again. Why do you always have to screw things up?"

I turn and stalk down the lane. Away from the highway, away from my mother and her manipulating ways. I have second thoughts about leaving the car but locate the keys in my pocket. She'd probably go without me. When I'm around a jog in the road and out of her sight, I find a rock to sit on. A red-tail hawk swoops low searching for a meal, missing the gopher that signals a warning before diving into its hole. I run my fingers through my hair and find it sun-warmed. After ten minutes of blissful solitude, I head back. She — that woman I'm travelling with — has tidied up our lunch, no doubt emptying the wine into herself so the bottle wouldn't leak. She waits, arms crossed, foot tapping.

"You're such a miserable person, Edith, leaving me all alone. This trip was your idea, after all. I came along out of the goodness of my heart."

"'Goodness of your heart' is an oxymoron, Mother. Anyway, it's YOUR sister we're going to see."

"She's YOUR Aunt," she flounces. "And think of all the interesting people you've met."

"Name one."

"Walter," she offers. "Maurice? Charleen?"

"That's pushing it. I could have lived my whole life without knowing them and still be happy."

"Happy? You?" She rounds the back of the car. "Seeing as I couldn't be trusted with the keys, you can put the basket away yourself." She has left it on the ground.

"Get in," I direct, unlocking the trunk then kicking the rock from behind the tire.

Mother, instead of opening the door and doing what she's told, decides to park herself on the front bumper. She removes a shoe, shaking out a stone. The car shivers. Mum jams her toes into the shoe then pushes against the ground to wiggle the whole foot in. The thrust is enough to get a good downhill roll going. She grabs the edge of the bumper.

"Whoa-a," she commands, digging in her heels.

I step out of the way.

While Mother rides one end of the car, the other end hits the basket, mounts the side and stops on top, the tire settling cosily into the contents. I hear the snap of wine glasses and the rebuke of the Romanovs.

"Mother, could you push a little harder? You didn't quite complete the destruction. I think a plate is still intact."

"Edith, what have you done?" She bends over to examine

what used to be lunch. Her dirty hands slide down both cheeks leaving rust-coloured streaks. "You're in big trouble."

As I get into the car I notice the problem, a new one to add to the growing list. The gearshift has popped out of first. After warning Mother to remove herself from the road, I baby the stick shift into reverse and let the clutch out easy. The basket works better than the rock. The car doesn't budge. I put it into first and it moves, but not enough to dislodge the wickerwork. With more gas and determination, the car lurches forward with surprising speed. In the rear-view mirror a projectile much like a picnic basket vaults down the lane, tumbling end over end. I back up to where Mother now stands slack-jawed, viewing the remains.

"Your shoelace is untied," I point out.

My passenger slouches in silence but now and again inhales deeply, letting out a whining, lingering sigh. "On the Road Again" repeats in my head as the miles click over the odometer. Saskatchewan passes endlessly beside us. She sighs again at Gull Lake and indicates a service station.

"You wanna stop here?"

"That's why I pointed." Chilly response.

"Do you have a problem, Mother?"

"Other than you? Yes, Edith I have a problem. I have to pee. D'ya mind?"

The tires squeal as I round the side of the garage. The young man inside looks up from his magazine. A minute later he hears Mother kicking the locked door of the ladies washroom and, anticipating her next move, leans over the counter hooking the chained key on his finger. He swings it like a pendulum when she stomps, as expected, into the office. He playfully snatches it away before she can grab it. *Oh, kiddo, you shouldn't have done that.* He wraps it around his fingers and swings it again, egging her on. *You're dealing with an asp, kid.* She has him dragged halfway over the counter before he can loosen the chain from his hand. *That will teach him never to mess with a woman with a full bladder.*

Upon her return, she replaces the key on its peg, smiling at the boy as he cowers on his chipped wooden chair sucking his fingers.

"Nothing like inflicting a little pain to perk one up, eh Mum?"

"Who WAS that mauve-haired matron with the gold tooth, you ask?" She slaps her thigh making hoofbeat-like sounds. "Hi ho, Dixie, awa-a-a-a-y."

The crisis about the picnic basket has passed for the moment. It will rise again when we turn over what's left to Vonnie. Mother hums as she studies the road map. "Let's stop in Swift Current and find a store where I can get a few clothes. Maybe there's a Harrod's or Saks."

"How about the Co-op? Or K Mart?"

"Maybe we can hit a garage sale, or rummage through dumpsters." She's heavy on the sarcasm.

"Hey, good idea. Now you're talking."

"Edith! I want to wear something nice to meet Vonnie. You might do the same."

"No, thanks. Not interested."

"Don't be hasty. He might be just what you need."

"Excuse me, Mother, but I don't NEED anyone."

"He owns a car dealership that was written up in the Guinness Book of World Records."

"Was not."

"Was too."

"Why?"

"You'll see."

ANTELOPE. WEBB. BEVERLEY. Mum reads me the roadsigns as they flip by. Family farmhouses occupy tidy parcels of land. A progression of poplar trees, turning gold with the season, border the gravel lanes. In the distance a pair of railway engines sing siren-like, luring a caravan of boxcars westward. SWIFT CURRENT.

"See, Mum, there IS a Co-op. Your big chance."

◥

"Look!" I shout, taking my gaze from the highway. "Pense!" I signal and pull over onto the shoulder.

"Jeezus, Edith, you scared the hell outta me. What are you bellowing about?" She fans her face with her hand. "Why are you stopping?"

"That's Pense." I point out the window, across the highway to the town.

"So what?"

"That's where Joe Fafard lives."

"Who?"

"The cow man. You know ... ?"

"That enlightens me a whole lot."

"Do you remember when Sears was going to do a fashion shoot in Saskatchewan? When western wear was in?"

"No."

"Yes, you do." I know I told her, but she just doesn't listen. "This is where they were going to come. 'Til it snowed."

"So what's this got to do with Joe Foofer?"

"Joe Fafard sculpts the most wonderful cows. Toronto has life-size bronze ones just lying on the grass."

"Saves on feed, doesn't it?"

"I wonder if he's home?"

"He's not." She taps the steering wheel. "Let's go."

"I bet if I turn around and drive through Pense I'll spot where he lives. Probably has a big neon sign — HOME OF JOE FAFARD."

"And it's blinking CLOSED ... CLOSED." She flashes her fingers.

"Mother, you have no appreciation of art."

"Since when did you become so artsy-fartsy? You still have paint by number pictures hanging in your bathroom."

"They have sentimental value 'cause Dad helped me paint them. Anyway, that's beside the point."

Mum raps her fingernail on her watch then holds it to her ear. "Time is of the essence ..."

"This will only take a few minutes."

"Are you gonna buy one of his cows, or what?" she asks irritably. "And where are you going to put it? Up front? I'll just sit in back with the canning. After all, I'm expendable."

"I'll see how much they are first."

"Why don't you catch him on the way back. It's too damn hot now."

"True," I admit, grinding into first. "Anyway, there won't be canning on the trip home. We'll leave it with Queenie. With Joe Fafard's cow in your seat, you'd get the whole back to yourself."

Easing onto the road, I watch Pense grow smaller in the dusty side-view mirror. "I'll drop in on the way home."

"Well, maybe I'll fly instead," she threatens. "No doubt you and old Bossy can do without me."

Ahead, Regina's buildings shimmer mirage-like on the horizon. On the outskirts of town, Mum clears her throat. "Think we can stop for a drink?" she broaches.

"I thought you were busting your ass to get moving?"

"Edith. You sound like a fishwife."

"Are you in a screaming hurry or not?" I ask, annoyed.

"If you didn't argue with me so much, I wouldn't get thirsty." Mother coughs again. "Just a small drink. To settle the dust."

"Look for a McDonalds or 7-11."

"Not a wussie drink. I want a cold beer."

She won't return my glare. Anything to keep her quiet.

A sideroad into the city leads to a shopping centre and as luck will have it, a neighbourhood drinking establishment.

Inside it's dim and surprisingly busy for the early hour. Aside from smelling like stale cigarettes, it's pleasant with the late afternoon sunshine glinting through stained glass windows.

Mum pulls at the front of her new dress pumping cool air over her chest. A bandy-legged waitress in a cinched-up peasant blouse struggles over to lean against our table.

"You ladies seen the sign?" she asks around her gum.

"Sign?" I reply.

"The sign what says LIVE DANCERS."

"What other kind is there?" asks Mother.

"LIVE DANCERS EVERY THIRTY MINUTES?" she repeats.

"I think she's trying to tell us we're in the wrong place, Mum."

"Nonsense, Edith. Order a beer."

"Listen to her, Missus. You don't b'long here. The older ladies usually have tea in town at the Inn."

That does it.

"We'll have two draft, Toots," Mum orders, getting comfortable.

"The show starts in ten minutes. You gals be done by then?"

I nod. Mother says, "We're here to stay."

As my eyes become accustomed to the shadows, I realize that aside from the two waitresses in their push-up bras, we are the only females in the pub. The men, a grey lot, tilt back in their chairs, most with an arm too casually thrown over the back. They don't look at us directly but dart furtive glances, checking us out.

"You quaff it as fast as you can," I warn, when the drinks are slammed down mid-table.

"Gives me hiccups doing that." She inclines her head and lifts her glass, acknowledging someone's salute from another table.

I'm almost finished my beer when the commotion starts. Angry voices swell over the hum of listless conversation. A bar stool topples to the floor. Mother stands to see what's happening. I tug on her dress, but she pays no notice, her neck craning toward the fracas. "Looks like a fight," she says eagerly, squinting into the thick atmosphere. As she's about to climb onto her chair for a better view, a man bulldozes his way through the drinkers, directing himself to our table. Mother is caught with one foot hoisted onto the seat and one teetering on the plank floor of the pub.

The man, unshaven and red-eyed, moves quickly behind throwing an arm about mum's neck. He grabs my glass and whacks it against the edge of the table. It breaks away in a spray of beer, leaving in his fist a lethal weapon.

I can't believe Mother just asked him what the hell he thinks he's doing.

I should rescue her, throw myself before him and say take me instead, but I don't. My bowels are turning to water and my shoes have grown into the floor.

"Shaddup, lady," cautions the man to Mother, now his hostage.

The grey men circle our table. In back of them, strobe lights blink in time to the sudden pounding of music. A red-haired dancer wearing little more than a six-foot python, struts onto the stage in her exaggerated heels. She starts her routine and only notices she is without benefit of audience when the bartender dismisses her with a slashing sign across his neck. She shrugs and minces off, throwing the snake around her neck like a feather boa.

"You ashholes," the hostage-taker slurs, "have been meshing with me long enough." His knees buckle but he regains his balance, the hand still gripping the glass. *Oh, god, no blood.* He shifts my mother from his front to the side, which she will be thankful for later, as the crotch of his pants is ringed with urine stains. The men watch, leisurely finishing their beers.

The feeling returns to my body. "Let her go. Please." Nobody hears and I really can't tell if I actually spoke until Mother rolls her eyes toward me.

"Hey, man, you gotta bitch with us, come outside," says a guy in a plaid shirt, now that he's finished his draft. The others nod in agreement, shuffling their boots.

"I'm keeping her 'til I get my money." He lifts mum's face

with a forearm held beneath her chin. "Maybe might have to kill her."

There's an excited pitch to the hum. I think this bunch would enjoy the change of pace. The bartender replaces the phone and edges toward the door.

"For chrissake, lemme sit down," Mother protests.

"You talkin' to me?" the man asks, loosening his hold in surprise.

"Yeah, I'm talking to you. You're sucking me out of my new shoes."

"Jeez, lady, I'm shorry." He releases her, brushing his grime from her back. "Not yer fault." He pulls out the chair and holds it for her, then collapses to his knees and finger dusts her pumps.

"What would your mother say, assuming you had one?" Mum chides, wagging her warning finger.

The hand still holding the broken glass is brought up abruptly when the door bursts open and two Regina city policemen push their way in. The man lumbers to his feet and rests the bottom of the glass on Mother's shoulder. He turns to face the advancing officers.

"Billy, Billy, Billy, what th' hell are you up to now?" asks the older one, removing his hat to wipe his sleeve across his forehead.

"I'm taking me a hoshtage."

"Be careful with that glass, Bill. Don't want anybody getting hurt," the policeman cautions as the uniformed pair casually splits to stand on either side of my mother and the man.

"Fer sure," he says, straightening the jagged weapon.

"Anything we can do for you, Billy?"

"Yeah, order me two beersh. Two."

"Then you'll let the lady go?" the officer prompts.

"Might. Might not."

The cop indicates that I'm to leave the table. I get up slowly so as not to startle the man with the pissy pants but he doesn't notice. "Know what?" he says, bending over to bury his nose in Mum's hair. "You smell nice. Like a real lady."

The younger cop carries from the bar two drafts of beer

then slides them onto the table, pushing them toward Billy who downs the entire contents of the first glass. He wipes his chin on his arm and belches wetly.

The older cop makes a move but stops short as Billy tilts the shattered glass toward Mother's ear.

"All right, Bill. Fun and games are over. Guess we'll have to shoot you."

"Gimme a match. Somebody gimme a match," says Billy flipping the stringy hair off his forehead. A book of paper matches is tossed on the table. "Now gimme my money or the lady gets it."

"Drop dead," says the guy in the plaid shirt.

"I warned ya." With that, he pours the remaining beer over Mother, then releases both glasses to reach for the matches. He strikes one and yells, "Stand back or the lady burns."

⚜

Once again we're on the highway driving east. The wailing continues as she blots herself with brown paper towels, dropping the used ones into a wet pile around her feet.

"Are you going to carry on like this until we hit Manitoba?" The pitch of her whining hits a higher frequency.

"I was almost murdered," she trumpets. "Brutally assaulted." She rubs the back of her grazed right hand absently.

"Your knuckles still hurt?" I ask.

"A fat lot you care. Quit laughing."

"I'm not really laughing. Didn't anyone ever tell you to hit *above* the buckle."

"It didn't come to mind. I just wanted to deck him," she answers heatedly. "And I did a damn fine job."

"Why didn't you press charges instead?"

"The guy is a schmuck — a loser. It's you who should be charged."

"Me?" I shrill.

"Yes, you!" she says flinging a wadded paper towel into my lap. "Taking me to a place like that."

"That does it. That bloody well does it. You're on the next Greyhound. Better yet, you're UNDER the next Greyhound." I pull to the side of the road then notice the entrance to a hospital parking lot. Once in there, I turn the car around, cross the highway, and head back to Regina.

"Edith? Edith? What are you doing? You're being belligerent, aren't you?"

"Where's the bus depot?" I call out to the car beside me at the first set of lights. They point and I wave thanks and head in that direction.

"Edith! Don't go off half-cocked. I've had a terrible experience and now you're being mean to me. I wish Walter was here," she moans.

"So do I." *Never thought I'd say that.* My resolve weakens and I draw into a parking spot before a pizza joint. "Granted, it was a harrowing experience with that drunk, but it was your idea to have a beer."

"Maybe."

"It was your idea to linger over that beer."

"Yeah yeah. Now look at me. The dress is ruined. My hair is hanging in my face and …"

"… and you stink."

"Is that why you've been driving with the window down?"

"Uh huh."

Beneath the stiffening mauve strands of hair, Mother's chin starts to quiver. The corners of her mouth turn up. I must say this in her favour — she has a wicked infectious laugh. People carrying out pizzas dip their heads to see what's going on inside the car.

"If Billy the half-wit thought I smelled good before, he'd love me now. *Eau de Molsons*. Positively orgasmic." She picks up the balls of paper towelling, exiting the car to dump the lot into the nearest garbage container.

I notice her sailor's gait as she walks away. One shoe is missing a heel. My mother looks like a dog's breakfast. When she gets home she should be able to dine out for weeks on her pub adventure. "Let's go find us a good motel in Indian Head," I say, lunging into traffic when I see a break.

"With a big bathtub," she adds, pulling down the mirror, "full of gin and ... oh my gawd!"

◢

"Aren't you just a little excited to be reaching Indian Head, Edith?"

"Well, seeing as I had no intention of stopping here, I guess you could call it exciting."

"Getting to meet Vonnie and all."

"And all what?"

"Oh, all that I have planned."

"What does that encompass, Mother? Do I behave like a princess or put in a diaphragm?"

"Don't be crass, dear. It's not becoming." She's looking me over with an inordinate amount of attention. "We'll do something with your hair later."

"MY hair? What's wrong with it?" As if I don't know.

"Nothing, dear, except for volume. The in-look is sleek this year."

"I am not now, nor have I ever been, sleek. I have hair enough for three people. I am perfectly perfect for the shape I'm in."

"Yes, dear."

Oh gawd, I'm doomed.

"Maxine said it was on this street. Drive down again." Mother has her head launched out the open window. "I think you just passed it. Stop! Back up."

"I can't back up. There's a taxi behind me."

"Oh, go ahead, back up."

I wave for the car to go around, then reverse until we're next to a weedy little hill sloping down to meet the sidewalk.

"That's it, Edith. Vonnie's!" She says this as though she's just won the lottery.

Atop the knoll is a scrubby building half the size of the sign it carries.

V & G MERCEDES SALES.

Strung from the corner of the metal roof to a post twenty feet away, faded plastic triangles try valiantly to be banners.

"This place is in the Guinness Book of Records?"

"Smallest Mercedes dealership in the World, Walter said." Mother slides from the car, quietly closing the door. "I'll surprise him." She chugs uphill toward the office.

"You'd better come back," I call through her open window. "We'll phone first." She waves at me to be quiet. "You're still a mess ..."

She stops dead, looking down at the front of her dress then briskly wobbles back to the car. Almost makes it, too.

"DIXIE? THAT YOU?" calls a speaker located on the lot.

She breaks into a run, attacks the door handle and jumps into the car.

"Go. Before he know it's me."

CLICK.

"Hurry up," she urges.

CLICK.

"The starter's gone," I advise, cranking the key.

"Gone? Gone where?"

"Just gone. Won't bloody well turn over."

"He's coming!" She sinks beneath the level of the window.

"Start, goddam it," I order. "Oh, my lord, is that him?"

"Try to be polite."

"Toad-like, isn't he? I'll bet there's not a fly within blocks."

"E-E-e-e-dith. He'll hear you."

His progress down the incline comes in a series of hops, for his thick bowed legs will not allow a leap.

"You can tell he's Walter's son, can't you?"

"Yeh," Mum agrees, raising her eyes to window level. "Sharp dresser, just like my Sweetie."

As he passes in front of the car only his head and shoulders show above the hood.

"Snile," she says, forcing the command through clamped teeth.

I do as I'm told and *snile* at the face now leering in my window.

"Jeez, Maurice was right," he says. "Beautiful. Beautiful."

"Thanks, but it's been a long day. My hair's a mess."

"What — twenty-five, twenty-six years old?" he asks, fondling the side mirror.

"I'm fo … late thirties."

"He means the car, you nit," Mother hisses.

"I'm Vonnie." He stands on tiptoe to poke his arm into the car. "That your mother?" He points to her back.

"So I'm told," I reply.

He retracts his extended arm, resting it along the window opening. Mother makes herself as small as possible by hanging over her knees. I run my hand down the prominent backbone bumps just as you'd do to your favourite old hound.

"You lose something down there, eh, Dix? Lose something?" he repeats, sniffing loudly. "She drunk?" he asks. "Drunk? Want to lay her out in the office 'til she sobers up?"

Mother rises like a phoenix. A dignified sweep with the back of her hand removes the beery hair from her face. "Silly me, ah lost mah compact," she says with a Blanche DuBois drawl.

"She okay? Drink of water?" he whispers into my neck. "Water, maybe?"

"Ah'm splendid, just splendid," she insists.

His shoulders shrug to his fleshy ears. "Maurice said two wonderful women would show up on my doorstep and here you are, eh." He studies himself in the side mirror, then pulls his tie into alignment. "Here you are."

"Yes," says Mother entering into the listless conversation, "here we are."

Now what? I wonder.

"Now what?" he asks.

An uncomfortable silence swells before I plunge in. "We should find a motel for the night."

His eyebrows lift, bringing his face along for the ride. The beginnings of a leer.

"MOTHER and I." *Idiot.* "Something reasonable and clean. With towels," I bumble. "And soap."

"Well, lovely ladies, you're in luck, eh," he crows. He bobs up and down on his toes, Walter-like. "There's a place right down the end of this road." He points out the direction. "This very road. Cheap, clean. Frock House."

"Thanks, Vonnie. What'cha waiting for, Edith?"

CLICK. CLICK. CLICKCLICK. CLICK. CLICK.

"Starter," he diagnoses. "Lift the hood, eh."

I release the catch and Vonnie raises the front.

"This is so embarrassing," I whisper earnestly.

Mother sucks her tooth as she peers through the crack between the dash and the hood, watching Vonnie in action. "Try to be helpful, Edith. Hand him tools or something."

Reluctantly, I leave my four-wheeled sanctuary. Vonnie stands on the front bumper pressing his suit jacket to his chest so as not to get it dirty. The free hand is prodding at the bunched wires.

"Can I help?" *I hope I don't sound too sincere.*

"Think it's just the electrical. Engine's dirty. You gotta shampoo it, eh. Wash it."

"Yeah, right," I scoff. "Maybe a perm and a tint, too?"

"This baby's a piece of work, eh, worthy of your undivided attention." His body wavers, finding its balance. "Focus." His hands cut from his temples to the motor. He repeats the gesture, echoing, "Focus, focus."

"Look, Vonnie, the only thing I want to focus on right now is shampooing my Mother. Will the car start or not?"

"Yeah, yeah. Try it." He steps off the bumper, impatiently waving his dirty hand.

"Try and start it, Mum," I instruct through the side window.

She turns the key from the passenger seat and the car bolts forward, still in gear. The open hood jaws shut inches from Vonnie's face.

"Jeezus H. Christ! You women are an accident going somewhere to happen. Christ." In his anxiety, he leaves a perfect imprint of his palm on the front of his shirt, three greasy fingers on the collar, with the pinkie finger extending to the lapel of the green suit.

He really should avoid green.

Mother, oblivious to the near disaster she's caused sees me laugh and assumes she's missing out on a good time. She smiles and leans on the horn beating out a tattoo. This latest indignation is too much for Vonnie, who stumbles over the curb in his haste to leave.

"Thanks, Vonnie," Mother calls to his retreating back. He flaps both arms in acknowledgement as he climbs to the safety of his office.

She leans out the window to holler, "Can we buy you dinner?"

"No," I insist as I slide back into the car.

"No," he yells from halfway up.

"I think he likes you, dear."

"How could he not, Mother? How could he not?"

A stuttering pink neon sign reluctantly reveals the whereabouts of the motel Vonnie promised.

"Frock 'ouse," she says unexpectedly.

"Beg pardon?"

"The sign," Mum points out.

Foot-high letters flash FROCK -OUSE, FROCK -OUSE,

FROC ... as we turn into the gravel driveway and stop. It's a typical U-shape motel with a garden of cement and marigolds in front of all the units. Only one other vehicle is in the parking lot, a white van with a screaming eagle airbrushed on the side panel. Smaller lettering on the door reads "the DINKMEISTER".

Before I can get the car into reverse, a thirtyish, pinch-faced woman bangs open the office door. She clamps her arms over her stomach as she walks a rigid line in our direction. I can hear her narrow body bend as she speaks into the car's interior. "Welcome to our little establishment." The greeting falls like dry leaves.

"We're just looking." The gearshift knob vibrates in my hand. "Aren't we, Mother?"

Mum bobs her head in agreement.

"You the ones Vonnie Muckle just called about? From Vancouver?"

The tightening at the back of my neck sends out a warning jab. I could have gone on a cruise. Singles week to the Caribbean. Mai Tais, dances, movies, lolling about in the sun. Motherless.

We nod.

"Room Three," she says pushing the key in through the window.

"Where's that?" asks Mum reaching past me to take it.

"There," she points, "Between Two and Four."

"Everything in its place," I say.

The owner dips her head in accordance. "Bible's in the drawer. Services in our chapel behind the motel are held Monday, Wednesday and Friday, every three hours, starting at noon."

"Park anywhere here?"

"... and if I might finish, on Tuesday and Thursday evenings it's Ladies' night. Bread and water served. A token, you understand."

"I don't ..."

"Then," she bulldozes, "THEN, Sunday we devote the day. Different testifiers on the half hour. You look like you might have a story to share. Have you come from a life of Hell? Damnation? DRINKING?"

"She's talking to you, Mum. Tell her about your time in Attica."

Mother answers with a slap to my thigh.

"Ahhhh, I knew it," says the Frock House evangelist. "Salvation is at hand." She rockets her arms into the air dropping her head back to look heavenward. Across her throat I notice a faint white scar extending from left ear to right.

I interrupt her exaltation to again ask where to leave the car.

"Right next to the van," she says crossly, holding up her blade-like hands. Anything less than neat parallel parking will be frowned upon.

"Looks like we're here for the night, Mum," I say, as the woman cuts her way back to the office. "Want me to try another place?"

She shakes her head then holds up her hands as if in prayer. "I feel the call, Edith. I FEE-E-L THE CA-A-L-L-L. Where's the bathroom?"

"Gotcha."

While Mother takes the key to open Number Three, I remove my suitcase from the trunk. It's looking roomier now that the Aunts have ownership of the dried flowers, golf clubs and Mother's baggage. She's travelling with just her Co-op dresses.

Once I reach the cement entranceway I drop the bag onto its three wheels. The fourth revolves with no regard to the direction of the rest. In front of Number Seven, a man silences the strings of his guitar to watch. He nods at my glance, then continues strumming. Long dark hair shields his face.

Our room smells like bleach. Pseudo-oil paintings of the harvest are bolted to the wall. By throwing her shoes on top, Mother has claimed the bed closest to the bathroom. "You want in here before I have a bath?" she asks, poking her head around the bathroom door. Behind her, the ceiling fan clunks with every revolution. "No? Then can you find me something to wear? Something tatty of yours will be okay."

That lets out the strapless chiffon.

The water pipes hum as Mother fills the tub. On the remaining bed I throw my suitcase and sling back the top. A long blue shirt and knee sox should do her.

"Where's the underpants?" she demands after fielding my choice.

"You can't have them. They're brand new."

"So much the better."

"No way."

"C'mon, Toots," she wheedles. "Want me to wander around with my bum hanging out?"

"Don't care."

She gives me a one finger salute before retreating back into the steamy bathroom.

The motel windows are painted shut with the exception of the one at the head of my appointed bed. There's no bar and no fridge, only a TV that takes quarters and I feel like I'm getting my period. I hope I can adjust to all this excitement. I reluctantly head out the door to approach the musician. "'Scuse me?" I mumble. "'Scuse me?"

The chording stops and he flips back his hair. I ask if there's a liquor store nearby. He sets the guitar just inside the door of his unit and steps off the stool, stretching.

Guys that wear open shirts and gold chains generally have an attitude. He's probably no exception. From one belt loop of his tight faded jeans he undoes a leather thong. He drapes it over his shoulder while he gathers his hair in a ponytail behind his head. My gaze drops to his button-up fly.

"Kind of gets to you, doesn't it?"

"What?" I jump.

"The place," he indicates with a sweep of his arm.

"Oh yeah, the place."

"A liquor store, huh?" He chews at his long thumbnail then realizes what he's doing and drops his hand, shoving it protectively into the top of the jeans.

"Just need a bottle of gin," I explain. "Uh, a small one for my mother." I limply indicate door Three.

"Yeah, I had me a mom like that, too, until the accident." He looks from number Three directly at me. For the first time I notice he has one blue eye, one green. Weird.

"Go down a block, next to the Christian book store. You'll find it." As he inclines his head in the direction I'm to take, his earring flashes.

Bet he has tattoos.

"Thanks." I walk away knowing he'll be watching my rear end. "Thanks, again," I repeat, turning sharply to catch him in the act. The doorway's empty.

When I return, gin bottle in a plain brown wrapper, our proprietor, Ms. Frock House, rounds the registration desk flapping a piece of paper.

"You've a message," she calls sullenly from the open screen door.

"I do?" I shift the package guiltily. "From who?"

"Whom," she corrects, folding the paper before handing it over. "From our Vonnie." She backs inside, then speaks through the screen. "Says he's sorry. About what, I can only surmise," she sniffs. "And ... AND, he says he'll behere-aboutsixtotakeyoufordinner."

"Pardon?"

"I said ... dinner. At six. With Mr. Vonnie Muckle."

"Me?" I have a sinking feeling.

"'Those two', is how he put it." She returns to her desk but not before reminding me to register NOW, as she needs time to prepare her Scripture before the next gathering.

"I'll just see to my mother," *and put this gin away.* "Be right back."

"M-U-U-U-THER!" I bellow.

She exits the bathroom with puffy whitecaps foaming on her finger waves. "I tried your mousse."

"So I see. Here's your booze. I gotta check in." I duck out the door, then step back in to announce, "By the way, your impetuous dinner invitation has been graciously accepted. Himself'll be here at six o'clock. Thanks a helluva lot." I pull the door hard to punctuate my last remark. The knob comes off in my hand. When Mother yanks the inside knob a hole appears in the door. I peer in as Mother peers out. It's not often that Mother and I see eye to eye.

Seconds later she opens the window above my bed and heaves the other half of the door knob into the scrubby marigolds.

"Get me outta here. Don't you walk away. E-E-E-dith!" She hoists my borrowed shirt to throw a bare leg over the window ledge.

"Alright! You win, take my underwear." Has anyone else seen more of Mother than is necessary? The musician's door is closed, and I don't hear anyone calling the authorities.

At the office, a sign on the screen door invites potential guests to "ASK AND THOU SHALT RECEIVE. RING AND WE SHALL RUNNETH OVER." Our landlady must be out back delivering the message. Once inside the office, I see our card atop the registration book on the desk and fill it in, spelling my name EDYTHE, just to add a little lustre to the mundane.

By reuniting my half of the doorknob through the hole with Mother's returned half, and wiggling the pieces until something clicks, we engineer the door's reopening.

"Did you bring tonic water for the gin?"

"I thought your getting out of this room was the priority, Mother," I say primly.

"Well, it was. The next crisis is no tonic water." She embraces the glass holding two fingers of gin.

I quarry through my loose change looking for loonies. "If I buy the mix, you realize there won't be enough change to run the television."

"Don't worry about the television, I have a safety pin."

"A safety pin?" I puzzle. "Never mind, I don't wanna know."

"... and ice," she reminds my retreating back.

Chauffeur, hand-maiden and now butler. *Yes M'lady.*

"Don't slam the do ..." My counsel comes too late, as the knob drops onto the stoop, rolls slowly down the first two steps and comes to rest on the third. This is lunacy. Madness!

And I am in Indian Head, Saskatchewan, all because my brother-in-law Bernard makes damn good blackberry wine.

In a fury I stab the chrome buttons of the telephone next to the ice maker then pick paint flakes off the wall while I wait.

"Collect to Vancouver." They are bloody well going to find out what it's like. I read the walls. FOR A GOOD TIME CALL PEARL.

"From her sister, Edith." She bloody well *better* accept it. Tell *her* a thing or two. She sounds so chirpy on the other end.

"Vern-n-a-a-a?" I wail. "She's awful. A shrew. A bitch. A harridan," I under-assess. "She's wearing my clothes, my underwear, my nerves to a frazzle ..." I whine.

"Poor me, is right! She's also met a man! A cheese salesman. And had a run in with a hostage taker in a bar ..."

"No, Verna, the cheese salesman didn't take her hostage. A drunk did. Different guy."

"No, it didn't turn out alright. HE GAVE HER BACK."

"It's not funny. Now, now we have to go for supper with the son-of-a-cheese-salesman. I wanna come home."

"Well, no, it hasn't been all bad," I begrudge. "We did go bowling with the Aunts. Octogenarians in fluorescent tights ..."

"Yeah, yeah, I'll finish what I started," I promise reluctantly, "and carry on to Coolish. What more can she do? Right? Right?"

My sister sends Mother her best.

"You realize, Verna, that you'll pay forever?"

After hanging up on my link to normalcy, I take a minute to search for solace in the ice machine, inhaling the cool interior, then scoop a paper bucket through the crescent-shape crystals. Metallic pounding echoes around the motel. It's coming from the direction of number Three. Now what?

"I fixed the knob," she says proudly, giving one last glancing blow with a rock. She squats to replace the stone at the garden's edge.

"Gawd, Mother, don't bend over." I warn, shielding her from the rear. "There may be women and children about."

"S'all right. I'm decent. Your underwear covers me from arse to armpit." She dusts her hands together and mounts the steps. "Tonic water?"

I hand her the cans in answer.

"Atta girl."

My gin and I head for the bathroom and a tub of hard Saskatchewan water.

By the time Mother bruises the door, waking me up, the water is cold. My neck is cramped into a question mark. Even the smallest movement trails streamers of pain. Must come from the gravel I hear grating inside.

Seeing my reflection in the mirror means I won't be giving off a look of indifference. The angle of head on neck gives the effect of perpetual curiosity. Like a robin tip-toeing through grass, listening for dinner below his feet.

"You die in there, Edith?"

"What time is it?" I call, over the suck and gurgle of draining water.

"Five to six."

"Aww, Jeez!"

I bend forward gathering handsful of hair, sweeping up any strands that get away. The steam has kinked and twisted the mass into something with a life of its own. The mirrored results are disappointing. When reassembled the topknot of hair is clumped to the opposite side as counterbalance to the tilt. A thirty second application of makeup and I come out of there looking as though I just spent the better part of a full minute pulling myself together.

"Oh, spiffy," says this well-groomed purple-haired, Co-op dressed woman. She resumes blowing on her freshly polished nails. She looks up again, lines corrugating her forehead. "What?" she asks testily. "What?"

"I didn't say a thing," I reply, turning carefully to rifle in my suitcase. *Surely my lady-in-waiting packed the black Dior.* I just can't seem to find it.

"Then stop doing that," she says, mimicking my neck

spasm. "You look as if you're waiting for me to answer."

"Gee, Mum, I kinda like this look. Gives me the opportunity of looking up taller peoples' noses."

Shave-and-a-haircut rapping heralds Vonnie at the door just as the six o'clock news comes on. Precision of that sort is annoying. Mother entertains while I dress in the bathroom.

"Hi," I say as I emerge.

"Hi," he responds, bobbing on bent knees, not sure whether he should stand or remain sitting as I make my grand entrance. He genuflects twice more then falls back into the chair. His pink scalp shines through raked over hair. "You look very … um … interesting. Yeah, interesting."

"She's put her neck out, poor baby," says Mother, feigning concern. "Want me to rub it?" Sounds like a threat.

"Sports injury?" asks Vonnie. "You a jock?"

"No, I don't want it rubbed and no, it's not a sports injury. I'm a jock if soaking in a tub is considered a water sport."

He gropes for ice in the drink Mother has provided. "We could put on a cold pack, Edith. Might help," he offers. Water from the melting ice slithers from his hand, down the length of his polyester pants onto his maroon cowboy boots, ending in the orange shag carpet.

"No. It'll be okay, thanks." I run my knuckles over the stiffness. *Sure it will.*

Vonnie throws the cube into his mouth crunching and grinding until dissolves. "Wanna stay home? Stay here if you're ailing?"

"Edith's a real trooper." Mother jauntily slings her purse over one arm and opens the door. "Aren't you, dear?" She indicates which way is out and as we file past, she gently shuts the door behind us.

Ms. Frock House leans against her screened office door, watching our approach.

Vonnie pauses briefly. "Thanks for passing on the message, Junie. Thanks, eh."

"Sure. And have a real nice supper." The mock-sincerity is chilling. She crooks a finger at Vonnie as we go by. He returns to stand in front of her. Without unfolding her arms, she leans to whisper curtly, "THIS...TOO...SHALL...PASS."

Does she mean my affliction or the evening?

Mother locks onto his arm when he rejoins us. "Is there a problem?" She tips her head toward the office.

"No. No. Junie and I once had an ..."

"Oh, I see," says Mother, jumping in.

"... an understanding. Once. Long time ago."

"I gotcha," says Mum ardently with a 'nudge-nudge, wink-wink' look. "So, Vonnie, where's your car?"

He doesn't answer until we hit the gravel area. As there are only two cars in the lot, I sort of suspect the worse. It's either his vehicle hunkered next to mine or Junie is preparing an evening requiem for a newly departed soul.

"A hearse?" Mother screeches.

"S'okay, Dix. S'okay. There's no one in it," he says heartily, "'cept the goat, eh."

I yelp as Mother steps back onto my foot. My neck, poor thing, tries to straighten in defense. I'm afraid my blaring scares the hell out of the goat, for it leaps from the back seat into the coffin-holding area, and repeatedly rams the back window.

Vonnie ducks inside the cavernous car to quiet her. Kneeling on the rear seat facing backward, he strokes between her yellow eyes. "You've never done that before. Never. You love to ride in the car, don'tcha? You love it," he says solemnly to the animal.

"Gee, Vonnie, you gotta get that ... uh, goat stuff off the windows before it hardens," says Mother, always helpful.

"Never mind, Dorothy, you're a good girl." Vonnie chants to the goat as he backs away. "A very good girl." He closes the door quietly. Cupping his hands around his eyes, he peers inside the hearse. "Stomach must be upset." He taps on the glass. "Did they upset your tummy, Dorothy?"

He turns on his heel, facing us, one finger raised, mouth open.

I'm braced, ready to hurl back his abuse, but instead he breathes deeply, his checked shirt rising and falling with deliberation.

"This afternoon ... this afternoon," he soldiers on, "I figured we got off to a bad start, eh. I said to myself, 'try again', I said. Now, you've done this. This!" Vonnie throws open his stubby arms. "You startled Dorothy. What did she ever do to you? She's a lamb, that goat. A lamb." He starts to pace, hands clasped behind his back, head down. "I promised my brother I'd show you around. Promise is a promise, right?"

"Uhhm-m-m-m," we agree.

He continues, mimicking Maurice's voice, "'Take the two women out,' he said. 'Dixie's lots of fun. Fancies red garters and cheese.' Says Pop's smitten with the little lady."

Mother rolls her eyes then busies herself dusting off her bosom.

"What red garters has to do with cheese, I don't know," he admits. "Just don't know, eh. Pop used to be so rational."

I back toward the motel, hoping to escape while he parries and thrusts.

"So!" he finally announces. "So, now we go for dinner. Yes?" He forces a big salesman's smile on his face and clasps Mother around the shoulder. She tries to pull away but he has her firmly under tow. "Come, Edith. We will try again. Come." He holds open his other arm for me. It partially encircles my waist. "We will walk. Walking's good, eh?" *This from a car dealer?* He stops. "One minute," he requests, dropping the embrace long enough to roll his car windows down a bit. Through the open space, Dorothy fits her snuffly nose. Vonnie plants a kiss on it.

"Want to take the Mercedes?" I ask hopefully. "Your type of car."

"Nope. Only 'bout a mile."

"A wh-a-at?" Mother stumbles over the grass edging the sidewalk. "It'll be dark when we come home."

"Safe as a church here. A friggin' church." He gives us both a squeeze.

I extrude myself from his grasp and trail behind. From the back Vonnie and Mother look like Munchkins, which reminds me, "Why do you have a goat called Dorothy?"

"Need milk in my coffee. Milk on my Shreddies. The name," he shrugs, "came to me in a whirlwind." Speaking to Mother he adds, "V & G Mercedes Dealership. She's my partner. My silent partner, eh. Vonnie and goat." He chuckles at his own joke and gives her a fierce hug.

The Rainbow Room is a welcome oasis. We obediently wait inside by the sign that tells us to do just that. There are perhaps thirty tables. With our entrance, some of the diners look up acknowledging Vonnie with half-hearted waves.

"Hope our reservation is still good," he says checking his watch. "Eh?"

"Won't really matter, will it? The place isn't full." I notice a few people pointing me out over their shoulders, imitating my kinked neck.

"The folks that run this place are peculiar about house rules. Bit peculiar."

We're escorted to a table next to a small stage. Choice seats, the owner says, cause Vonnie's such a fell swella. It's true, I heard him say *fell swella*. Vonnie seats us, then excuses himself to table hop.

"There's no way on God's green earth I'm walking back. You can either call a taxi or an ambulance, but I ain't hoofing it," Mum complains. She signals the owner to order a drink. "Double G and T and the same for her." When he leaves, she lays her head on the table, arms hanging limply from the shoulders.

"It'll be the death of you," I caution.

She sits up with a sigh. "Can't come too soon."

I pat the back of her hand as Vonnie joins us, and behind him the waitress, menus pressed under one butterfly-tattooed arm. "Hi, again, Chickies. Want your bill?" she asks.

"We came for dinner, Patsy. Just this minute got here," says Vonnie reaching for the menus. "Just a sec, eh."

"Suit yourself, luv," says Patsy, placing a pencil behind her ear. "It's surf and turf night," she announces, looking over our heads to a blackboard. "That don't mean water and grass." She whistles a laugh through her teeth, nudging Vonnie.

Mother and I smile politely, then duck behind our menus.

"I'll have what the ladies are drinking." Vonnie indicates our gin and tonics.

"Sure, luv. Be right back."

"So, whatcha having?" Vonnie asks, plunging his napkin into the collar of his shirt. "What looks good, eh?"

"No road kills," Mother warns.

I try to find her leg to give it a kick but she's too fast.

"If you're unhappy here, Dixie, we can leave," says Vonnie formally. "We'll go, eh."

"Nah, s'okay," she replies. "It's almost ... homey."

Patsy appears and slides a cup toward Vonnie, sloshing coffee over the rim onto the saucer, then departs.

"I thought you ordered a drink," says Mum hoisting her sweating glass.

He tips the contents of the saucer into the cup. "This'll do, this'll do."

Patsy, returning full steam, manoeuvres through the room holding a plate on high. When she berths next to our table her free hand snaps the napkin over my lap and she's about to do the same for Mother.

"I got it, Toots," says Mum, unfolding her own.

Situating the plate in mid-table Patsy is triumphant, "Here's lovely bread and butter." The order pad from her apron pocket is at the ready and the lead of the pencil licked. "Want your bill?"

"We haven't ordered yet, Patsy. Haven't ordered." Vonnie raises eyebrows in our direction.

"We'll both have the Special," I direct. "Medium-rare."

"Pancakes don't come medium-rare, luv," Patsy says, as if speaking to a fragile mind.

"This is the DINNER hour, Patsy," reminds Vonnie. "Supper, eh."

"Oh, sure. You want supper, right?"

"Right. Three Specials." He holds up three fingers.

She grabs them and kisses his ear. "You're a good boy, Muckie."

"Is Patsy slow or something?" I ask Vonnie when he

reaches for a piece of buttered bread.

"She's okay. Had a motorcycle accident a while back. Never been the same since. Just not the same, eh? Memory comes and goes depending ..."

She's back. "Three Specials, right?" She rubs her forehead vigorously with fingers missing two tips.

Vonnie nods. "Headache today, Patsy? Sore head?"

"Yeah, it's coming on. Must be a storm brewing. My plate's picking up the static." She taps the side of her head with the end of the pencil. "If that ain't bad enough, this damn tooth," she leans forward hooking the corner of her mouth with a finger, "is accommodatin' the radio station. Lotta flute playing." She straightens, wiping her finger across her puffy bosom. "Ready for dessert?"

"AFTER dinner." says Vonnie.

"Oh, right. Three Specials." She leaves for the kitchen, each foot planted steadfastly.

"The accident?" I ask. "Is that why she has no eyebrows?"

"And what does she mean about a plate?" Mother whispers, leaning Vonnie's way.

"The eyebrows were ground off in the gravel. Plate's in her head. She forgets things. Depends on the weather. All depends, eh." He dips a corner of bread into his coffee, chews the wet end and continues. "She picks up baseball broadcasts in summer with that tooth. I think she gets hockey in the winter, but she doesn't work then. Too cold on her head, eh. Too cold."

The Rainbow's owner arrives at the table. "H'lo ladies. Hear from Junie at the motel you're from Vancouver." After collecting our responses he turns to speak to Vonnie. "Jim, the plumber, from over at Jim's Humming and Pleating? Said he's waiting on a new car from you?"

Humming and Pleating?

"Due any day, Bubba. Should be a beaut. A beaut."

"Good man." Bubba mounts the stage to drag a short microphone to the middle. He clicks it on then taps until it whistles.

"What's happening?"

Vonnie ignores me.

Bubba blows into the microphone, not satisfied it's working until it shrieks. "Fifteen minutes to the eight o'clock fow, sholks," he huffs. "Starring ... OUR OWN ... DI-I-INK MEISTER.

After a patter of applause, Bubba leaves the stage. No longer master of ceremonies, he becomes lighting technician and in his hands a single spotlight chases around the restaurant.

"Bubba's our Mr. Show Biz," Vonnie says without apology. "Mr. Biz."

In answer to the cook's bell in the kitchen, Patsy hoists a tray to shoulder level. She looks toward our table plotting her course.

"I guess I'm hungry after all," I admit as our dinner arrives.

Curtsying with the weight, Patsy sets before each of us a seashell of considerable size. Steaming inside is a chunky chowder with crouton life rafts.

"What is it?" Mother asks.

"I dunno," answers Vonnie. "Beats me, eh."

"You ordered Seashells." She flips open the order book stabbing the page with her finger stub. "Three Seashells. And, Omar was really ... now what did he say? Wait a minute." The chef's white hat snaps up when she reappears at the kitchen. A raised cleaver hastens Patsy's return to our table. "Omar said he's seriously pissed. Ordering clam chowder. Tuesday is clam chowder day, he says, not today."

"We didn't order ..." begins Mum contentiously.

Vonnie grabs her upraised hand forcing it to the table. "I'll handle this," he says lowering his voice. He suddenly stands. "Tell Omar tough sh ..." He kneads the back of the chair while his lips move soundlessly. His self-counselling works, for he just as suddenly sits.

"'Scuse, ladies." His smile is a non-renewable resource. "Patsy, give Omar our apologies. Our apologies, eh."

She pushes on her tooth, then spins away complaining about a Mariachi band.

The eight o'clock show starts at eight-ten with the dimming of the house lights. The microphone waits mid-stage, mid-spotlight. A recorded drum roll ends abruptly when the needle is none-too-carefully removed. Bubba bounds onto the first two stairs leading up, catches his patent leather toe on the third and windmills into the light. "Stepid stupe," he complains looking back at the offending tripperance.

"Friends, neighbours, the Rainbow Room is pleased, nay, DE-E-LIGHTED, to present the one ... the ONLY ... MR. EXCITEMENT HISSELF ... DINK MEISTER." He invites an ovation.

Trudging up the same three stairs and ambling across the platform comes the eight o'clock show. He pulls the mike from the light into the dimness outside the circle. Off stage, Bubba issues a muffled oath on his way to re-adjust the beam.

The spotlight narrows, missing Mr. Entertainment entirely before swelling to a glaring embrace. With everything to Bubba's satisfaction, he heads for the bar where he backs onto a stool, hangs his elbows on the counter, and clasps his hands over his belly to watch the show.

The accordion is lifted to the chest of Mr. Excitement. His long fingers drift silently over the keys before he opens the bellows.

Mother leans against me to say, "Since when is an accordion considered entertainment?"

Something familiar about the guy on stage.

"NOT 'Lady of Spain'!" Mother complains, throwing herself against the chair back.

"Shhh!" admonishes Vonnie, yanking the napkin from his shirt front.

Dink Meister is grinding out a five minute Latin-American version of 'Lady of Spain' when he abruptly switches to a polka.

"He forget the music or something?" Mother quizzes.

"A medley," snarls Vonnie. "He's playing a goddam medley."

"I knew that," she snaps.

He's beating "Lucy in the Sky with Diamonds" into submission when a flip of the hair reveals the face beneath.

"That's ..." I point out, "that's what's-his-name from the place."

Mother reads her watch.

"The guitar player from the motel. You know?"

"Really." She doesn't even feign interest.

Vonnie places both hands mid-table, and rises to lean into Mother's face. "SSSHHHHHH!" His thumb leaves a deep imprint on the last piece of buttered bread.

"Hey, Vonnie ..." I begin.

"Don't defend her." He turns, fixing me with those bulbous eyes, now narrowed, "You and your stupid neck are just as bad." He sits down, wheezing. "Worse, even."

So, I won't tell him his jacket's in the soup.

After his waltz rendition of "Hava Nagila", the accordionist pauses, arms open, wrists limp, to bathe in the warm response.

Mother stands, "Well, that was sure nice. Gettin' late."

"Sit down, eh, he's only just begun," Vonnie says enthusiastically.

Bubba is suddenly behind Mother's chair. "Thank you for that, Missus. His first standing ovation." He looks a bit teary. "His mother and I are so proud."

Not content with assaulting our ears with his accordion music, Dink — Mr. Fun — polishes a mouth organ on his sleeve. He sets it into a chin level wire I had mistaken for a orthodontic appliance.

What seems like days later when the show is over, Mum and I head for the washroom. Dink and Vonnie are speaking as we return.

"Here's my girlies," Vonnie cries possessively.

We stay beyond reach. "Come meet Dink. He's giving us a ride home. Eh, Dinkmeister?"

Dink nods in our direction before snapping the accordion into its velvet-lined mausoleum. *May it rest in peace.*

"Maybe we should just get a taxi. Shouldn't bother you," I mumble into my shoulder.

"Suit yourself." He grips his instrument case and jumps off the stage.

"Hey, hey, Dink's my main man. Eh, Dinko?" Vonnie grins, back-slapping.

"Right," affirms Dink blandly.

"C'mon ladies, let's hustle. Shake a leg." Vonnie leaves a two-dollar tip between the salt and pepper shaker and picks up the bill. "Treat's on me," he says loudly. "On me, eh."

The musician leads the way, we benignly follow. In the parking lot is the van we saw at the motel earlier. *Was it only this afternoon?*

Dink slides open the van's side door to stow the accordion. Vonnie takes the opportunity to climb in, settling himself against the far window. Dink takes the driver's seat which leaves Mother and me to shift for ourselves.

"Excuse me, Madam, may I see you to your seat?" I bow deeply in Mum's direction.

"Why, you're too kind, ah'm sure," she replies, extending her hand.

I fasten her into the front then climb into the rear, sliding the door closed.

"You women's libbers don't still expect doors held open, do you?" Vonnie mocks.

"Not from the likes of you." *Now drop dead!*

As if to grant my wish, Dink pulls from the parking lot directly into the path of an oncoming car.

Showers of stars pinprick the night as the oncoming car collides into the van between Mother and me.

"What the hell … ?" Dink yells.

Someone's wailing.

When the tilt-a-whirl comes to a standstill, I run my hands over my face to see if it's still there. A sticky lump rises through my eyebrow. The stars stop falling.

The wailing from somewhere and everywhere now

undulates. Flat-nosed faces press against the windows.

Vonnie, wedged between the front and back seat, climbs my leg in a struggle to right himself.

Within minutes, lights alternately colour the van red, then blue.

"You guys okay?" Dink yells.

Vonnie returns heavily to his seat. In the pulsing party colours he checks his hands, finger by finger, flexing his shoulders and neck before answering, "Maybe ... maybe."

Dink persists, "How 'bout ... you?" We've never even been introduced. He can't say, "'How about you, Miss Flood?'"

"Banged my head, I think." *Sure as hell hurts.*

Someone outside reaches in to turn off the ignition. "Hey, man, you okay?"

Dink shrugs, "Guess so."

"Couple more in the back," the man calls out to the ambulance. "Gimme a flashlight."

He shines it over the van's interior and I shield my eyes against the intrusion. The beam hitting the front seat pales against the dazzle from the street. My mother's head slumps over the restraints of her seatbelt. My heart stops.

"Can you slide out so we can get at the old lady?" the man asks Dink.

A rasping wounded howl. Make it stop. Make it stop.

"Jesus Christ, lady!" The light hits my eyes again. "It'll be okay. Quit screaming."

He's mistaken. I haven't moved. Haven't opened my mouth. He reaches over the front seat to undo my seatbelt. The disturbance stops.

"See, you'll be okay." He swings back to look into Mother's face.

"Need a stretcher here," he charges, "and a collar." He holds back Mother's hair to look into her eyes.

"Leave her alone!" I strike out, dislodging his hat. "Leave my mother alone."

The van's back door shrieks open, metal against metal.

At the hospital on the outskirts of town, we're each taken to curtained-off spaces with little more than a bed. Mother, still silent, is wheeled to another area. They say I should just rest and wait for the doctor.

I feel there's no way I can rest, not knowing, but when the light shines in my eye, it comes as a surprise.

"Can you stay awake, hon, until the doctor's finished?" asks the person on the other end of the beam.

She sure smells nice. Like cotton candy. "How's my mother?"

"Was that the older lady brought in with you?" The nurse arranges pillows behind my back. "Oh, she passed, hon."

She passed on?

"Here's a cold pack for that eye."

Mother died? I've run out of air. "She ... died?"

"No, no, hon. Battered and bruised, maybe, but not dead. She'll be okay in a few days."

I cry anyway.

From the bathroom mirror, an apparition glowers back at me. Bonded to the bump by too much surgical tape is a gauze patch. *Where was I when they put that on?* Beneath the bandage, where my eye used to be, a mature avocado. I should have a headache that fills this hospital room, but strangely, I don't.

"Miss Flood?"

I open the door at the nurse's call.

"Hi, hon. Want to see your mum before shift change?" She holds a ratty blue robe for me to hide in. "Got a comb to run through your hair? Don't want to scare the poor woman."

My shoulder is unforgiving. Can't reach high enough to do anything.

"Sit down, I'll fix it." She pulls the hair up and back. "My goodness, there's a lot here. Elastic okay?"

I nod and feel the pull of the tape on my face. "Is the bandage for the bump on my eyebrow?"

"Just covering the stitches." She pats my shoulder letting me know she's finished.

"Stitches?"

"Two or three." She holds the door open.

Before entering Mother's room, I take a big breath and can't help but notice that my ribs hurt too. Must remember not to sneeze.

Chrome siderails enclose the bed where Mother makes a meagre outline. I resist the hand on my back urging me forward.

"Go ahead." The nurse checks her watch. "I'll be back in five minutes," she whispers.

After she leaves I shuffle to the bed in my paper slippers. Mother is on her left side, facing away. An extra blanket is tucked over the regulation threadbare one. "Mum?" The slight rising and falling of the covers is the only movement. *She's probably on life-support.* "Mum?"

"What?" she answers groggily.

"You okay?"

"Would I be here if I was okay?"

I circle the bed. The covers are tucked to her chin.

She briefly raises her head from the pillow. "You look like hell."

"Gawd, I was so scared." My chin wobbles and Mother reaches over the bars drawing me towards her. We touch foreheads. "I thought I'd lost you."

"They said you were sleeping," Mum says thickly, "but I

figured they lied." She traces my bandage with a finger. "I told them not to bother saving me." She wipes at her eyes with the sheet, sniffing back tears. "They wheeled me to your doorway in the dead of night to shut me up."

I sag into the chair next to the bed. I don't understand why I'm crying.

"I'm so dry," she says, extending a hand to the pitcher of water on the side table.

I pour some then slide my arm beneath her shoulders to raise her head toward the glass. She feels more fragile than I remember. Like the translucent bone china cups Verna and I used when we had tea parties.

She sips at the tepid water then fades back onto the pillows, breathing harshly. "Everything hurts."

"I know," I respond, stroking the arm outside the blankets.

"To add insult to injury," she continues, "during the endless night I'm sure I saw your father."

"A reunion, huh?" I've heard of that — bright lights and tunnels and loved ones waiting.

"Reunion, hell," she snorts, sounding more like her old self. "Pushed past me to get to Carmen Miranda. Sucked the cherries right off her hat." She taps the chrome bedrail. "Can you get this thing down? I can't see you through the bar."

I can't move it. "Did you get hurt much?"

"There's something wet and heavy across my stomach."

When I lift the covers I'm surprised to see a cast from her elbow, down. "You broke your arm?"

"I didn't break it. That idiot driving the van broke it."

"Time's up, hon," says the sweet-smelling nurse, poking her head around the door. "Almost breakfast. You can visit again before you go home."

"Home?"

She signals me beyond the door.

I trail my hand over the bed as I shuffle past.

"You'll be able to leave after rounds," the nurse advises, showing me out. "Your mother will be here another day or so."

"What about the two guys? Vonnie and what's-his-name?"

I ask as she walks me to my room. "And the people in the other car, the one that hit us?"

"Mr. Muckle and Mr. Meister," she counts off on her fingers, "were only shaken up. No injuries. Mr. Muckle did complain of whiplash so we supplied him with a collar. The kid that hit you was apprehended. Stole the car in Regina. He ran a stop sign. Had his seatbelt on, if you can believe it."

"Always the way, huh? Appreciate your help."

She waves off my thanks and returns to the nursing station.

My clothes from the night before hang in the closet. Blood from the cut on my head stains the blouse. I rinse it in the bathroom sink then drape it over the cold radiator. The doctor and breakfast arrive at the same time. I'm to be released before noon.

On the way to the motel, the cabbie hits every bottomless hole pock-marking the streets of Indian Head. Vonnie must have picked up his hearse and goat, for our Mercedes is the only car in the parking lot. Not a big night for Junie's business either.

I fight with the door handle to let myself in. No brass band to welcome me, no mother to say, "Gin and tonic, Toots?" I drop my purse and gingerly arrange myself on the bed. Should turn on the TV to kill the silence. I roll off the bed onto my knees. Must remember not to do that again. Poor knee, all black and blue. Most everything on that side is black and blue. In this position, I reach my purse and empty it. In the rubble, six quarters, enough for an hour and a half of mind-numbing television. The picture on the screen and my right leg are the same colour.

Somebody's thumping on the door.

The quarters have run their course and the TV screen is blank.

"Who is it?" I answer, not fully awake.

"Dink."

I can't tell whether it's really him or an anatomical insult.

He partially opens the door, and I, with a minimum of grace, sit on the edge of the bed.

"Saw you through the window."

"And still you knocked?"

"Hey, I wasn't peeping. Just checking."

"You may as well come all the way in."

Magician-like, the hand hanging outside the door now proffers cellophane-wrapped flowers, the kind bridesmaids carry. "These're for you," Dink says, thrusting them at me. Silver and white ribbon ringlets spiral from the bouquet.

"What for?"

"For the accident." He offers them again. "Sorry."

"Wasn't your fault. Kid in a stolen car." I take the flowers, trying not to hold them as if I were part of a wedding party. "Thanks," I say, smelling the blooms.

"No big deal. They were on sale."

As I fill a tumbler with water, Dink, with an involuntary groan, settles into a chair. I turn off the TV and balance the flowers and glass on top of the set.

"The nurse said you and Vonnie were shaken up?" I take the bed again as I don't believe I could climb from the depths of the remaining chair.

He nods, "How 'bout you?"

I shrug, remembering too late my right shoulder. "I've got a headache. My eye hurts like hell. Bruises look worse than they are," indicating my leg. "Other than that, I'm fine."

"You're not supposed to say 'fine' until you find out if I'm sue-able."

"I'll keep that in mind."

He smiles a little, "How's your mum?"

"Arm's broken. I'll know more tonight when I see her."

"That's it? Broken arm? I thought for sure she was a goner."

"Me, too. I figured I'd be going home alone." I extend my leg which is beginning to ache. "She's a tough old bird."

"Listen, I'll leave," he says, noticing my discomfort. "You probably want to rest."

"You seem to be sore yourself," I remark.

"Yeah, seat belt." He pats his chest. Didn't lose his gold chains though. "Anything I can do for you?" he asks, after working his way from the chair.

"Got any aspirins at your place?"

"Sure. Anything else?"

"New eye?"

He throws up his hands on his way to the door. "Sorry."

It's too soon to lay down if he's coming back so I limp stiffly to the bathroom, deliberately avoiding the mirror. My blouse, still not clean, and Mum's dress soak up the water drip-dripping into the discoloured sink.

This time he waits for me to answer the door. He comes bearing 222s, a bucket of ice, and a box of chocolate chip cookies. "This should help your eye," putting down the bucket, "your head," placing the 222s on top of the ice, "and your stomach."

"Thanks ..."

"No problem," he insists as he departs through the still-open door. "How are you getting to the hospital tonight?"

"Uh ... haven't really thought about it."

"I'll drive, if you like," he says brightly, "you being banged up and all."

"Thanks, that's ... very nice. Six o'clock?"

"No problem. Glad to see you trust me with your car." He steps outside, closing the door.

MY car?

By the time I reach the door he's gone, but arriving in his place is Junie.

"What's going on here?" she says, arms clamped over her chest. "You're entertaining men in the unit? It's not allowed. Rules."

"For your information, madam, this room is rented to me." *I should have taken those 222s.* "My visitors are my business." I step forward invading her space. "Is that clear?" The hammering surges behind my eyes.

Junie backs away, dropping the subject. "What happened to your face?" she says stiffly.

"Car accident." I reply, taking a small comfort in feeling for the bandage. "Last night."

"Would you like a healing service?" she asks optimistically, holding both hands near my head. "I feel a lot of heat. All down the right side."

Her hands follow my outline, and it's my turn to step back. "No, thanks."

Her eyes forge sparks, "I could bathe you in the restorin' light of the Lord."

"Save it for Vonnie."

"Vonnie? My Vonnie?" Those healing hands cross over her heart.

"He was in the same accident. And my mother, and what's-his-name. Lives over there, Unit Seven."

"Denis? He's injured, too?" Clearly she sees another soul chalked up on her salvation blackboard. "Duty calls," she charges, letting herself out.

Sorry, Denis.

After three hours with a towel of melting ice, my cyclopic eye acknowledges that in ten minutes Dink will be here and I'll be relinquishing my car keys. I confront the mirror and, like the looking glass in Snow White, it doesn't lie. *I AM the wicked witch.* I peel the bandage now drooping with the weight of accumulated water.

Left-handed, I tighten the ponytail made eleven hours before. It's not a pretty sight. A little lipstick and mascara and a brief spray of Mother's Cloe. Taa-dum! *Don't you dare cry.* So what if they shaved off half an eyebrow. I gain more forehead. Earrings, that'll pull the whole look together.

As Dink — *Denis* — is not as punctual as Vonnie, I have time to change into a long roomy charcoal skirt and a big red cotton shirt. I wash down more 222s and eat a handful of cookies. When I see him crossing the grassy area, I limp to the door with Mother's cosmetic bag and my cumbersome purse. I wait a moment after he knocks so as not to appear over-anxious, then slip my sunglasses on.

"Madam, your chariot awaits," he leans against the doorway, freshly shaven with a dab of lather still sticking to his ear. The hair is gathered in the same leather thong and tucked inside the collar of his pink shirt.

"Can you read minds?" I ask. He's on my left as we walk to the car.

He switches sides, then replies, "Don't think so. Why?"

"No reason." *A new shave AND a pink shirt. If he knew I find that a tempting combination ... too bad he's so young.*

"Any tricks to driving this car?" he asks, seeing me into the passenger side.

"She's plain and simple. Steering by armstrong." I turn on the radio, voiding the silence. Radio's still not working properly. So ... I think of clever, amusing things to say.

For miles.

"Do you have a real job?" I finally blurt.

"I play gigs."

"Gigs?"

"Mew-see-cal hennter-tainn-mint," he says in a Lawrence Welk imitation that sounds too patronizing. "You know, 'turhnn on ta bubba ma-sheen'".

My conversational skills exhausted, I face the side window. *Jerk!*

"And what do you do?" It sounds forced.

"Copywriter," I state. *Did I remember deodorant?*

"Pardon?"

"Copywriter," I say loud enough to restart the throbbing in my eye.

"Okay! Okay!" he says, taking both hands off the wheel to feign warding me off.

"What's a copywriter do?"

"You really want to know?"

He shrugs.

"It's for your had-ver-tising henn-ter-tainmint."

"*Touché*." He stabs himself in the heart with an imaginary dagger.

A cease-fire is in effect until the parking lot at the hospital.

"Are you always this crusty? Edith-isn't-it? Or are you pissed off that I tried to kill you last night?"

I hold out my hand for the car keys, then limp away muttering.

He catches up looking genuinely surprised. "What did you say?"

"It's an action verb. You figure it out."

Just walking from the parking lot to Mother's room loosens my knee and by hooking my right thumb into the waistband of my skirt, I can take the weight off my shoulder.

Flowers, enough for a state dinner, are banked along the floor below the window. "Wow! Who from?"

Mum is propped in bed, pillows mounded around her. The newly set arm rests on another pillow across her lap. Someone has brushed her hair and clipped a barrette to one side. She appears tired and wan.

"From Walter," she says listlessly. "Vonnie told him." She raises her good hand, then drops it. "How you doing?"

"Pretty good. Only half of me hurts and my neck is better. See?"

"Take your sunglasses off. Lemme see that eye."

I come closer. She has an abrasion on her ear I hadn't noticed before.

"Did you drive here in that condition?"

"Sort of. I'm not your only visitor." Denis leaves the open doorway where he's been waiting.

She turns her head at the sound, and her eyes suddenly blaze. "DINK!"

"I don't think she's calling my name," he teases, jamming the fingers of one hand into the top of his jeans.

"His REAL name is Denis," I advise.

"One N or two?" she asks, insolently. "I knew a two-N Denis who killed his brother with a baseball bat."

"In that case, one." He fingers his gold chains. "And I don't have a brother."

I give the cosmetic bag to Mum. She's perked right up. A little testosterone in the same room will do that for her. Can I find her mirror? Did I bring her lipstick? Did I bring her new dress?

After coyly asking Denis to turn his back, Mother awkwardly applies uneven blush and a wobbly line of lipstick. She requests a pen so he can sign her cast, even though it was he, "naughty boy", who put her in this predicament.

Vonnie's unexpected arrival in a purple jogging suit — a scarlet cervical collar restricting his limited neck — puts

Mother in great spirits. She beckons me over, no doubt to gloat over all the attention she's garnering.

"Look at him!" she whispers, indicating Vonnie. "Like a newly circumcised penis."

The guys think I'm having a seizure. It hurts so much to laugh I crumple over the bed on top of Mother's legs. She absently pats my back. Vonnie teeters on the edge of a green plastic chair waiting for the right amount of time to pass before fleeing.

"Vonnie," I say, finally pulling myself together, "I see you hurt your neck."

"Severe whiplash," he reports, as if his lips hurt too. "Lotta damage, lotta damage, eh."

"The nurse said you and Denis were only shaken up," I bait.

"Whiplash has been known to fell many a good man."

"Ahh," I say wisely, as if I believed. "How's the goat today?"

"Dorothy?" he replies. "Poor Dorothy worried the lining off the roof of the car. She's home resting." He grimaces as he tests the mobility of his encased neck. "Home, where I should be."

Mum tut-tuts in all the right places.

Vonnie steals ever closer to the door. With the corridor but a few steps away, he turns painfully. "Where you getting the van fixed, Dink? The van, eh?"

"It got towed to Honest Bob's. Need it tomorrow for my next gig." He looks at me, "I mean my next musical event."

"Honest Bob's?" barks Vonnie, then winces. "Whattabout my place? Eh?"

"I just don't like women mechanics, Muckie." *That thud was him dropping down another rung.*

"Loretta's not a woman. She's ... Loretta." *Him, too!* "C'mon, man, we gotta talk, eh. Gotta talk."

"S'cuse us, ladies," Dink says pleasantly, rolling his sleeves one more turn, "this is guy stuff."

Vonnie's cowboy boots clunk down the hallway.

Avoiding the elaborate flower arrangements, I watch the parking lot from the window. Only one of Mum's gentlemen visitors exits. "I have a feeling we won't see Vonnie again."

"You never even gave him Maurice's picnic basket," Mother reminds.

"That is why we're here, isn't it? Damn well forgot all about it."

"I wonder if the Romanov's put a curse on those wine glasses?" Mum rubs her one-signature cast.

It's actually the second-to-last time we see Vonnie, for when Denis and I return to the motel, Vonnie's hearse is parked under the trees, with Dorothy leaning out the open window to reach the lower leaves.

Denis locks the car, hands me my keys, then thumbs towards number Three, "You got anything to eat in there?"

"Cookies," I answer, "and gin."

"You eat like a musician." He's about to say more but I cut him short.

"I'm not hungry, anyway. Thanks again. See you tomorrow."

He looks through me with his unusual eyes, then wheels without speaking and walks to his unit, head drawn into his shoulders. I fumble in my purse until he's gone, then unlock the trunk of the car. Jammed into the middle of the spare tire is the basket. With no one in sight, I carry the remains to Vonnie's car.

"Hello, Dorothy. Nice goat." She relinquishes the leaves to sniff in my direction. When the rear door of the hearse opens she backs up suspiciously, head lowered. I waste no time in placing the basket over the seat into Dorothy's territory, then amble to the office.

"Excuse me," I call from outside the screen door. A brief shuffling from the back room before she answers

"Can I pay for another night, please? I'll be here until Mother …"

"Yes, I know," she says, opening a hairpin with her teeth and replacing it in her undone hair. "Let me check to see if your unit is still available."

Probably will be until next May. A head peeks around the corner of the same back room. "Hello again, Vonnie. Saw your car outside. You left without saying good-bye."

"Had to get a prescription filled." He points, "Neck."

"No, thanks, not tonight. I have a headache."

"Huh?"

"Never mind." I pay for lodging and when I turn to go, add, "Maurice asked us to leave his picnic basket in your good care, so it's tucked in the back of your car. Please tell him how much we appreciated the beautiful lunch." The door closes with a sigh. "G'night."

On my way past the mechanized social area of pop and ice cubes, I purchase dinner — barbecue chips and a Coffee Crisp. A spirited can of mum's tonic water should compliment the meal.

It's only after locking the door and pulling the green window blinds I realize I have but one quarter, enough for fifteen minutes of television. Rather have a hot bath anyway. I drop my skirt to the floor and step outside its circle.

The book I'm struggling to read closes and falls next to the bed. As I reach to turn out the light, there's a rapping on the door.

"Who is it?"

"Me."

What now?

I pad to the door. "Which me?"

"Dink."

"I'm in bed."

"Are you asleep?"

"Yes."

"Then I'll just leave all this stuff on your top step. Don't fall over it. Wouldn't want ..."

I slide the bolt and peek out.

"… you to hurt yourself. Can I come in?" he asks, holding up a covered tray.

"I'm not dressed."

"S'okay. I won't look." He closes one eye.

"Just let me get a sweater or something." It doesn't cover much nightgown but it sends out a message of modesty, whether real or imagined. "Okay, come in."

"Hell, Edith, you're covered. I figured you were sporting something small and see-through."

"My G-string's in the wash," I say, wrapping the sweater.

"Ah, yes." He carries the tray to one of the chairs. "I gotta put this down. It's heavy."

"What is it?"

"Breakfast. You can treat yourself and have it in bed. Unless you'd prefer being served?" he cocks an eyebrow.

"What's under there?"

He tents the white napkin then folds it neatly into a glass on the tray. "I brought fresh juice," throwing an orange and catching it, "just have to squeeze it. And a bowl of Froot Loops," he adds. "Well, it was either that or Coco Puffs," he says, seeing my look of uncertainty. He smacks his forehead, "That's it, isn't it? You'd rather have Coco Puffs. Knew I'd get it wrong."

"Froot Loops are … fine. Very colourful." I sit on the end of Mother's bed, clutching the sweater to me. He balances on the edge of the chair next to the tray.

"And," he taps the screw top, "a thermos of coffee. Black?"

"Perfect." I try to smile convincingly.

"Really? You take it black?" I nod. "Hot damn, I lucked out."

"Why are you doing all this?" I ask.

He ducks his head, hair falling over his eyes. He pushes it back indifferently. "I dunno." He stands abruptly, jamming his fingers into his waistband, "Stupid, eh?"

"Not really. It's thoughtful and I appreciate that."

"Yeah? If you're happy, then I'm happy." He bounces to the door.

I walk over to lock it behind him. "Thanks, Denis."

"Hey, no problem. What're neighbours for?" He hesitates after opening the door, starts to leave then changes his mind. Cupping my chin, he unexpectedly brushes a kiss on my bruised face.

"Your poor, poor beautiful eye," he whispers, then shuts the door on his way out.

It's too early to be gripping a bowl of dry Froot Loops between my knees or to be washing it down with lukewarm coffee but a blush of strummed guitar colours the morning. Denis is sprawled outside on my doorstep with his back against the door, playing the whole of West Side Story. *"Hi wan to leeve hin Amer-e-eca. Hokay by me in Amer-e-eca."* And ... he's not bad.

When I open the door, he rolls backward into the room, still plucking the strings. "'Mornin'."

"Likewise."

"D'you think I can have a cup of that coffee? It was the last I had."

"Tell me honestly, are you a danger to yourself or the community? Are you allowed to hold sharp instruments?"

"No and yes. Why?" he asks, rising, dusting himself off.

"Well, you bring me breakfast, play your guitar outside my door and now you're saying you gave up the last of your coffee. That in itself is almost a proposal of marriage."

"You're ... okay."

"That's it? I'm okay? My sister thinks I'm okay, too, but she wouldn't do any of those things."

"I'm not your sister. I don't like you like your sister likes you. Hey, I admire the sound of that." He taps his pockets. "Got a paper and pencil?" He repeats, "I don't like you like your sister likes you" as he writes it down. "New song," he explains, slipping the paper under the guitar strings. "See, you ..." he falters, "you're kind of interesting. Sort of unusual."

"Your flattery is underwhelming."

"You got it all wrong," he says, pacing. "No, I've got it all wrong. You ARE interesting, not 'kind of'. You ARE unusual, not 'sort of', and that's what's okay." He helps himself to the thermos, pouring coffee into a glass. "I write soppy love songs but they're not real."

"Real?" I echo.

"Like you. You're real. I'd like to ... um, sort of see more of you."

"Pardon?"

"Well, not see MORE of you, you understand, but see you more."

"Like a date?" I ask suspiciously.

"Uh, well, sure. Whatever you want to call it," he says, looking into his glass.

"How old are you, Denis?"

"How old are you?"

"Well, I'm uh, thirty-nine?"

"That makes me uh, thirty-five."

"Quick, what year were you born?"

"Nineteen, uh ..."

"That's what I thought. Thirty-five, you're not."

"So?"

"You're much younger than I am."

"So?"

"It doesn't bother you?"

"Why should it? Younger, older, I don't go in for all that crap." He suddenly grabs the neck of the guitar. "Listen, forget it, okay. No big deal." Before he's fully out the door, he bumps into Junie. She enters as he heads out.

This woman has radar. I note her eyes darting to the unmade bed. "Your mother called," she says, fingering the buttons on her dress like a rosary. "She left a message for you. She's quite excitable, isn't she? Knows a lot of cuss words for a woman her age."

"She all right?"

"Says she can't get out until tomorrow and something about missing a birthday party."

"Shit!"

"You want the same accommodation?" she says, grimly ignoring what she sees as an inherited trait for profanity.

"I guess. One more night."

"Bless you. I'll write it up. Pot Luck Evening Service tonight. With your circumstances, just bring a dozen donuts or something. We'll pray for your mother's soul."

Junie, patron saint of lost causes. "Thanks."

After she leaves I try concentrating on an Anthony Burgess novel but my mind wanders. The headache has dulled. I should be working on Sears Spring catalogue, not lolling about in Indian Head. And I'm hungry.

In order not to frighten dogs and little children on my walk to the nearest convenience store, I hide my bruised legs in long pants and my plum coloured eye behind sunglasses. Mum will be so ticked off missing Queenie's birthday, I buy a jar of crystallized ginger to pacify her. I wash down a sandwich of processed cheese with warm cream soda while defiantly sitting on a bench clearly marked FOR QUICKY LUBE CUSTOMERS ONLY.

The motel room exhales warm air as I re-enter. In the mossy light begrudged by the green blinds, it takes on a look of the tropics. I would love to sleep naked for just one hour under a crisp white sheet that smells of sunshine. Sleep without interruption. But with Mum needing clean clothes and visiting hours just fifteen minutes away, I head for the parking lot instead.

A tapping on the windshield startles me.

"Why you sitting in there with the windows rolled up?" Denis calls.

I roll one down. "Never noticed." The keys are still clutched in my hand.

"How's the shoulder?" he asks, opening the door.

"I know it's there."

"Shove over, I'll drive."

"Don't you have anything better to do?"

"Well, I should be checking in with my parole officer." He looks happy to see my reaction.

He revs the engine twice before backing the car out. By the roadway near the motel sign he stops, pulling on the emergency. "Edith, I'm really here to proposition you."

Here it comes. How 'bout a quick roll in the hay. Wham, bam, thank you, Ma'am. "Oh?"

"Your mother won't be out until tomorrow and my van won't be ready for another year, so I wonder if ..." he releases the brake and continues down the road, "maybe I should drive you guys to Coolish, you still being injured and all?"

"What's the catch?" I ask, *brushing the hay off my damaged ego.*

"Catch?" he says, as if there wasn't one.

"Uh huh."

"Well, see, I have a gig near there tomorrow night at the Barrelhouse. I just thought ..."

"Let me check with Mum."

"Sure."

"... so, Mum, Denis here has volunteered to drive us to Queenie's so we can make the birthday. Whaddya say?"

"Come here," she commands, flicking her head.

As I near the bed, she grabs my t-shirt, pulling me close to her face with her good arm. "Are you sleeping with him?" she says too loudly. I glance up but he looks away, turning his grin into a quick cough.

"Don't be ridiculous!" I whisper earnestly, prying at her hand.

"Maybe you should give it some thought," she says sweetly,

smoothing the wrinkles she made in my shirt. "He's a hunk, just like my Walter."

"Mother, for chrissake, lower your voice."

"Edith, for chrissake, lower your drawers."

"That's it! I'm leaving. You're out of control again."

"Denis, may I have a word?" she says, slyly.

I head for the nursing station and learn the hospital is only too happy to discharge her first thing in the morning. *No kidding!*

"She should take it easy," the nurse is obliged to say, "and not get too excited. After all, a person her age ..."

I wait in the hallway, back to the wall, until Denis leaves Mother's room and saunters towards me. "She's incorrigible, you know," I begin when he's within hearing. "Strung out on pain killers. You really shouldn't believe a word ..."

"Aww, she's pretty cute."

"That's not how I'd describe her," I reply, turning to keep half a step ahead. He grabs at my elbow.

"O-w-w-w."

"Sorry, I forgot." He stops. "Slow down a minute. She's right, you know."

I wait for him to catch up. "About what?" I ask tightly.

"Damn near everything."

I don't trust myself to speak until we're inside the car. "What did she say about me?"

"It wasn't only you."

"Yeah, right."

"She said you live a solitary life. Needed a Walter in it."

"My mother is a manipulator and controller."

"And she thinks you are clever and beautiful."

"Oh, no, no, no. You made that up. She never said any such thing."

"And ... you're a good cook and would make a wonderful mother to the four kids you've always wanted."

"You're lying."

He laughs soundlessly. "She says there's still time, Edith. You're only ... thirty-nine."

I push as far into the corner as my shoulder allows. "Bugger off."

"Good idea. Matter of fact, that's what I intend to do after supper. I gotta work tonight at the restaurant. Want to come?"

"No way."

"Means having a hot dinner. On the house."

"How are you going to play the accordion with a sore chest?" I scoff.

"Not going to. I'm riding a pony bareback while juggling lemmings."

"Bareback?"

"Interested?"

"Wouldn't miss it."

I'm beginning to wonder if I didn't get invited to dinner just so Denis could get a lift to work. While we wait for traffic to thin before turning left into the restaurant parking lot, I note the windshield glass sparkling on the roadside, remnants of our accident the day before yesterday. It seems longer than that.

Even with his guitar case, Denis is quick to open doors before I do. I even give him the opportunity. We're no sooner inside when Patsy approaches.

"Hello, sweetheart," she coos, holding Denis' face with her hands and pulling him down to kiss his cheek. "Saved you something nice for dinner. C'mon."

"Talk about friendly service," I quip.

"Just like home," he says smoothly, following Patsy to a table tucked against the wall near the stage.

"Here you are, chickie. Don't know why I set for two," she says puzzled. "Am I supposed to eat with you?"

"Edith's with me. She was here the other night with her mother and Vonnie, remember?"

"Can't say's I do, but pleased to meet you anyway. My boy not treating you good?" she asks, looking at my eye. She pokes him in the chest with one of her amputated finger stubs. "You being mean to her?"

"No," he answers. "She was in the van the other night when the kid hit us with a stolen car."

"Is that true?" she asks, moving directly before me as if her nearness would prevent a lie.

"It's true. I hit the side window. It looks worse than it is."

"Oh, honey, I don't think that's possible," she says sympathetically.

Denis breaks in, "Edith, this is my Ma." He holds her around her shoulders and she beams with the attention.

"Your mother?" I repeat dumbly. She pumps my extended hand, surrounding it with her battered ones. "Pleased to meet you, Mrs. Meister."

"Oh, honey, I ain't been Mrs. Meister for years. Sit down and I'll bring you a nice cool beer."

"Your mother?" I query after she departs.

"Why you so surprised? We all have them."

"Vonnie never mentioned you two were related."

"Common knowledge."

Patsy leaves two cold bottles and two frosty glasses.

"Vonnie said she'd been in an accident?" I continue. "Motorcycle hit her?"

"Sort of. She was hit from behind by some drunk in a truck. Her Harley landed on top. Burned her pretty bad across the back, chewed off the fingers and crushed part of her skull."

"Jeezus!"

"But she's as tough as nails," he says, lifting his glass in salute toward Patsy waiting tables across the room.

"And she manages on her own?"

"Most times. I came back here to live after the accident. She needed some help until her brain rewired itself. Now Bubba has taken her on which leaves me more time for out-of-town gigs. They're living together in a double-wide out back of the restaurant. They seem happy enough."

"I take it she's given up motorcycles?"

"She still gets a certain look in her eye when one's parked out front."

Patsy appears behind Denis, hugging her arms around his neck. "'Nother beer, luvs?"

"Thanks, Ma. That'd be nice."

She kisses the top of his head then whistles as she scoops the two empty bottles from our table.

Later, with the restaurant patrons gone and the door locked after us, we walk across the vacant parking lot. "Cooler," Denis says. "Feels like the end of summer."

Inside the restaurant Bubba switches off the neon rainbow arching above my car.

"That was a grand show you put on."

"Why, Edith," he says with amusement, "you said something nice about me. That could be misconstrued."

"Must have the been the breaded oysters your mother laid on for dinner." We both stand before the driver's side of the car until I remember I'm a passenger.

"Thanks for the tribute," he says, "but I think you were in the minority, liking my guitar work. People still want me to squeeze out 'Blue Spanish Eyes'." He casually tosses the instrument onto the back seat. "So, what do you want to do now?"

"What do you have in mind?" I ask, getting in.

"Want to come to my place and see my etchings?"

"No-o-o."

"You can hardly wait to get home, eh? Drop a few quarters in the TV, wash your only glass? At least come for a drink. Be rash and reckless, stay up til 11:30. You're perfectly safe."

I snort my scepticism.

"What? You don't believe me?" He twists the rear-view mirror to reflect my face. "Until the stitches come out and the swelling goes down," his grin taking the sting from the remark, "believe."

"You have any cheap wine?" I return the mirror to its place.

"The worst," he says. "Drink it right out of the paper bag."

"Then I'll come for half an hour."

At his place, number Seven, a bongo drum acts as foundation cornerstone for scaffolding holding a collection of mouth organs in and out of their respective boxes, small percussive gadgets and a banjo. Three guitar cases on the floor function as footstools. A stereo system with coffin-size speakers defends its space against an encroaching bookcase, too small for the number of books. Expiring on top of this pyramid is a rangy plant, brown leaves curling around a fist-size figure of a sleeping cow.

After he pushes a perplexing number of buttons, his stereo lights up like a small city. "Do you want Michael Bolton or Whitney?" he asks.

"Bolton, I guess." The CD melts into mood music.

He prods an indolent cat from the back of the hide-a-bed. It's slept there before, as a lingering patch of grey fuzz will attest.

"I knew you'd be over so I tidied up," he confesses.

When he sees me start to bristle he quickly amends, "HOPED you'd be over. Hoped. Before I blow it, do you want a glass of that Saskatchewan plonk?"

"Not really."

"Cup of tea?" he says, heading for the kitchen.

"Sure."

"A guy has to be so politically correct nowadays," he explains.

"How so?" I clear a spot on the coffee table for the anticipated cup.

"Women don't want to be called girls. Can't hold doors for them. Can't pinch their bums anymore."

I react as he expects, rising to the bait.

"Sure miss that," he says wistfully. "Patting girls' bums."

I sit down again knowing I'm being had. "Instead of bum patting, you should spend more time gardening," I retaliate. "I think your plant has passed on."

"Maynard? Naw, he just wants sympathy."

"And water?"

"Watered him in August."

I can only shake my head. "You still want to drive to Coolish tomorrow?"

"I gotta go," he insists, intent on carrying the teapot and mugs. "It's a nothing gig, but Tizzie's counting on me to show. They had the Polka Czars booked but they cancelled at the last minute with some sort of emergency. I'm good at filling in. It pays the rent." He sets the tea on the table. "It's a good three hour trip so we gotta be on the road by noon."

"What time are you playing at the whatsis?"

"Barrelhouse. I always seem to be somebody's eight o'clock show." He angles forward to centre his tea on the floor between his feet, then reaches to remove the thong binding the hair off his face. "Damn hair was wet when I put it in this morning, now I can't get it undone." He drops his head to show me. "Can you get the knot?"

How many times has this line been used? Phone your mother.

He looks up with those unmatched eyes.

This isn't going to work, you know. I can see right through the ambush. Very unpolished. "I don't have any fingernails," I reply.

"My chest," he pats. "Pulls the muscles to reach up."

Try keeping them warm by buttoning your shirt. "Poor thing," I mock, but find myself walking towards him. He turns his back and I stand well away as I reach for the tangled piece of leather. He has this down to a science because it really is unmovable. I try to slide the fastening down but there's hair caught within the knot. It means moving closer to see what's wrong. By pushing the stiffened lace back through the knot, it loosens. The freed hair releases the scent of shampoo and cigarettes. It feels soft and warm in my hands. *This is entirely too pleasant.* "Here." I lay the thong over his shoulder as I had seen it the first time I met him. "I must go. We'll pick Mum up at the hospital then head out. That suit you?"

Denis whistles his breath between his teeth. "Whatever." He lifts the cup from the floor as I let myself out.

"Thanks for the tea. And supper. Give Maynard a drink, will you?" And I close the door on a golden opportunity.

◢

Junie is delighted to receive room payment this morning, but becomes drawn around the mouth when Denis carries our suitcases past the window. "Good morning, Denis," she calls but gets no reply. "He's where you are quite a lot the last few days."

"We're going to Manitoba. Together."

"Manitoba? How ordinary." Junie slams the guest book shut.

Today I don't care what June has to say. I feel great. I can actually see the blue jean sky with both eyes. Denis is morosely heaving the suitcases into the trunk. The guitar and accordion are stowed last, with more care.

"Well, I think that's it," I chatter. "Great day, huh?"

Denis gives Junie brief acknowledgement before leaving the motel lot. His thermos rests between the seats. It does feel good to be underway again.

I don't acknowledge his reticence until his one word answers become irritating. "What's your problem?" I finally ask.

"Not a morning person," he grouses.

"You were a morning person when you fell into my place yesterday."

He grunts unshaven behind his sunglasses.

Little boy didn't get his own way last night. I notice the same thong is back in his hair. Good for another try. We take an oath of silence for the drive to the hospital.

Mother is dressed and waiting impatiently in the lounge when we arrive.

"Stuff's in the room, Denis dear," Mother dictates. "Edith, pay the nice people, that's a good girl."

While a nurse-aide prepares to wheel Mum to the car, I head for the accounting office, chequebook in hand to wait out their coffee break.

When I return to the car, Denis is leaning against the driver's side, face to the sun. Without turning he says, "Check out the back seat."

Ivory gladioli curve gracefully above blushing roses, clouds of baby's breath and limp-wristed daisies. Enshrined among the banked columbine, a spray of lady's mantle fainting across her lap, is the dowager queen herself, pale against her pillow. She allows a common bearded iris to nuzzle her neck.

"I think we'll have to drive with the windows open," Denis remarks over the roof of the car.

"A bit overdone, don't you think, Mother? They won't ride, you know."

She sighs, raising the uncasted hand to her brow. "Take them away then, Edith. Just give them to the poor. The downtrodden. Walter will understand."

"The water in the vases will slop everywhere." I try to reason with her through the open window. She turns her head languidly to the side. "You're right, as usual. Leave them in the parking lot to die." I open the door to reach for the first bouquet. "NOT THE ZINNIAS," she wails, "Why don't you just rip out my heart."

"You said to leave them behind," I remind her sharply.

"And do I know what I'm saying? A poor, broken woman, dragged from her sick bed."

I slam the door and walk from one end of the lot to the other, and when I look back knowing what awaits me, I do it all again. Denis still doggedly faces into the sun sucking up those rays as if Mother and I aren't there. When I'm sufficiently winded, I mope back.

"Feel better?" they say in chorus.

"Oh-h-h-h, how I wish I was driving," I threaten, getting in. "I'd jackrabbit outta here and there'd be flowers stuck where the moon don't shine."

"Edith, how crass." She raps on the window, "Denis, dear, we're away. And ... drive carefully!"

Waiting for a break in the highway traffic, he pokes the radio buttons but only gets a metallic hiss and crackle.

"Sometimes it doesn't work," I admit.

One nice thing about the flowers, it muffles her voice. I hardly hear her say, "Where's Charleen when you need her?"

Three hours, four at the most and she's Queenie's problem. I will relinquish my duty. If I can find a wheatfield I'm going to sit in it and read a book.

⟁

"What did you do with your cat?" I ask.

"Huh?" says Denis, the question interrupting his humming.

"The cat. What did you do with him?"

"He's in back with the accordion." His early morning blue funk has dissipated, and in its place we get miles and miles of "Life is a Highway". "You know, Edith, I almost met Tom Cochrane once. Crossed paths at an airport. Winnipeg, I think. That's the kind of song I wanna write."

"The cat?" I persist. "And who is Tom Cochrane?"

"Not mine, and anyway I put him out. He wasted the cow," he answers. "Cochrane is a singer-slash-songwriter. You must have heard of him."

"If he's on CBC I guess I have," I reply vaguely.

"That close," he indicates holding thumb and forefinger together. "That close to the guy."

"That's ridiculous," I scoff. "How could that cat kill a cow?"

"What are you talking about?" He peers at me over his sunglasses.

"You said," I begin with a touch of annoyance, "the cat 'wasted' the cow."

"You're very strange," he says, giving me a brief unbelieving look. "The cat likes to eat Maynard's dead leaves. He likes the crunchy bits. Well, the next thing I know Kitty is on the shelf above the stereo and Joe's cow hits the floor. Kaboom!"

A prickle creeps up my neck. "Joe's cow?"

"Joe. You don't know him. A buddy of mine, Joe Fafard."

"YOU ... KNOW ... JOE ... FAFARD ... ?"

"Why, Edith, you're actually breathing hard. Is that what it takes?"

I check over my shoulder to see if his remark has been noted but Mother is dozing, mouth agape, eyes at half mast. "He's wonderful," I gasp. "I wanted to stop in Pense to see him, but she ..." I thumb to the rear, "wanted a beer."

"He lives in Regina. Just the foundry's in Pense. He's away at Duck Lake on a project. Be there 'til October."

"And you actually know him?" *It's okay that he doesn't like women mechanics. He has probably touched Joe Fafard.*

"Know him, worked with him, partied with him, what else?"

"And he gave you that cow?"

"He doesn't give his work away. I paid hard cash. Twenty bucks, anyway."

"And now it's broken?"

"And now it's broken." He laughs. "Don't look so grim. The world hasn't ended."

"I dunno," I say, shaking my head.

"Forget the cow. We gotta stop and get gas. Maybe fill this up?" He taps on the thermos.

"Sure. How about comfort food? Something greasy."

He pulls into the next service station and after gassing up we park the car at the side of the café. On the back seat Mother shifts in her sleep. Once we're at Queenie's we'll sit her in the sun. Get rid of those dark circles under her eyes.

"We're going for coffee, Mum. Want anything?"

"An African violet," she mumbles, pulling the pillow closer.

It's surprising what history emerges over a shared platter of chips and gravy. I find out Denis, an only child, doesn't know who his father is but suspects it might be the man he once called Uncle Spike.

"Your mother had a colourful past?"

"Sometimes she asks me about the 'Old Days'," he smiles, remembering.

"That's a switch, isn't it? You telling her?"

"I don't tell her everything," he confides. "She wasn't always Mother's Day material." He rubs his chin. "Jeez, I didn't shave."

A dusty yellow schoolbus pulls in, blocking my view of the car. "You weren't in the best frame of mind this morning," I remind him. A knot of road-weary kids begins to unravel around the end of the bus, lighting up stashed cigarettes.

"Sorry about that. I was pretty torqued you didn't stay last night."

"I don't do sleepovers." I gather crumbs and dust them from the table.

Denis folds his hands. "You're a very unusual girl. Can you sing?"

Before I can answer with a resounding no, the sleepy bunch of students becomes a screaming multitude, some reboarding the bus, others bumping into each other in their haste to enter the restaurant.

"It moved!" shrills a red-haired girl, holding her ears and twirling before the cash register. "It moved! It moved!" A strapping boy is only too happy to comfort her, even though a minute before he had elbowed her aside to get in here.

"Phone the cops," he says above the din.

"Let's go see what's happening," Denis says, grabbing the bill and his thermos.

"Phone the cops," the voices urge.

The agitated kids part, making way for the bus driver who leans across the glass counter to make himself heard to the cashier, then turns and holds up his hands motioning for quiet.

148

"Okay, kids. Knock it off." He swings to address the few customers inside. "Sorry, folks. Seems the students got a little excited over what they thought was a corpse in a Mercedes out there," he points. "All a misunderstanding."

I quickly push past the kids and wait outside for Denis. Passengers hang out the windows of the bus staring suspiciously into my car.

We feign a casual stroll towards the vehicle but it becomes a brisk trot as we get nearer. Oh, for a fast getaway.

"WHAT ... DID ... YOU ... D-O-O-O ?" I whoop, even before Denis hits second gear. He tilts the rear-view mirror to see her in her flowery bier.

"Can't a gal have a little fun?" she says, playful after her nap.

"Scaring children?"

"Lighten up, Edith. They're teenagers. It's not as if they're human."

"They wanted to call the police," Denis adds.

"Good for them," Mother says. "Make them take a little responsibility."

"What did you do?" I say more calmly. Maybe her pain-killers are doing weird things and she's not capable of rational thought.

"They piled out of the bus, OK? I was minding my own business, waiting for some sort of companionship," she begins, folding her arms across her chest, closing her eyes to reenact the scene, "when one of them looks through the window. He should have left it at that, but n-o-o-o, he had to yell, 'Look at the stiff!' Got a crowd then, but they didn't just look in the window, they stuck their whole heads in and one of them gave me a poke. So I opened my eyes and said 'bugger off'. And bugger off they did."

"Denis," I caution, "laughing will only encourage her."

‣

"Hey, there it is!" Denis says, pointing to the building set well back from the road. With the double rows of trees, I would have sailed right by without seeing it. He slows to enter the gravel driveway of the Barrelhouse and stops. "You be okay to drive to your relatives, Edith? Town's about three miles down the road."

I test my shoulder, "Sure, it'll be fine. I'll help you get your stuff."

We meet at the back of the car. He removes the instruments he'll be playing tonight and I shift things around so he can get at his leather backpack.

"So, Edith," he says, thumbs hooked into his pockets, possessions at his feet.

"So, Denis," I say, fidgeting with the car keys he's returned. Mother peers at us through the foliage in the back window.

"Will I see you again?" He grinds his heel into the dirt, making a puff of dust.

"We'll probably stop by on our way back home," I lie. "After three days here, Mother will be wearing a little thin."

"I HEARD THAT!" she yells.

I reopen the trunk to block her view. "I'll have to get the stitches out by then anyway." *In Vancouver.*

"This gig is for only one night and I'll catch the bus tomorrow morning. Gotta be back 'cause the kid's case is coming up."

Reminded, I feel my eye. "Okay then. See you."

He hesitates as if something is being overlooked, then throws his pack on his back, and picking up the battered music cases, trudges toward the rust-coloured building. The wind scrubs his footprints from the road.

I slam the door harder than necessary. Mum has moved into the front seat. "Don't say a goddam word," I threaten when I see her mouth start to flap. "You just point the way."

It's a quiet, perfumed ride through the town to the outskirts where Queenie lives.

◢

"So, where's the birthday girl?" Mother sings when Albert Fong answers her knock.

He shrugs and stands aside, the open door.

"YO-O-O-O HO-O-O-O, QUEEN-EE-E-E-e-e," she tolls, tracking through the house.

He returns to his *Winnipeg Free Press* crossword. An ashtray with four minuscule cigarette butts sits solidly on the arm of the green leather barber chair, a relic from his past. A leather strop still hangs from a silver hook on the back.

"She's not home. We've come all this way, Albert Fong, and she's not home."

There's no reaction behind the paper except a slight tremor of one leg.

"No decorations." She opens the refrigerator, but closes it before I can protest. "No birthday cake. NO NOTHING."

"Maybe we're interrupting," I say quietly, making my way past Uncle Albert to the door. "Let's sit in the car until we figure something out."

"Albert Fong? Albert Fong?" she shrills. We always consider his name as one word, joining it as 'Alberfung'. He turns a page, his leg more animated. "Thinks he's old-world aristocracy." Those are her parting words, as we quit the room, leaving the door ajar. He closes it before we reach the car. "He is the most infuriating man."

"Does he even remember you?"

"Oh, ho, ho. Yes. Did you see his leg jumping?"

A van rolls up, honking its horn. From the sliding door at

the side, a large equipment bag is thrown onto the ground, almost up against the picket fence; behind it emerges a person in a hockey uniform. As the van drives away, the hockey player in plastic-protected hockey skates duck-walks to the car .

Suddenly, the head inside the helmet pokes through Mother's window yelling, "HOWTHEHELLAREYOU?DAMN-NEARTIMEYOUGOTHERE, DIXIECUP!" all in one breath. "Somebody die?" The reference is, of course, to the backseat garden.

"Queenie? QUE-EE-E-N-EE-E-E?" Mother squeals, trying to open the door with her injured arm. Queenie jerks it open.

"Well now, look at you," she says, holding Mum at arm's length. "You play hockey, too?" she asks, rapping on the plaster cast with her knuckles.

"Car accident. Edith, too," Mother adds.

Queenie removes her helmet, tucking it under her arm. The electrical charge from the action makes her hair stand like copper quills. "Who's Edith?" she brays.

Story of my life ... who's Edith?

By pointing to the driver's seat, I'm acknowledged.

"Wow, what a mess. Nice mouse you got there," she says, tapping her own eye. "Your oldest, right? Where's the pretty one? The little ballerina?"

"Verna? Home with the kids. Edith here drove me out just for your birthday." She hugs her sister's padded shoulders, "Happy Birthday."

"Happy Birthday," I call joylessly.

"Thanks, gals. I'll just grab my bag and we'll have a cuppa. Why'n'cha go inside? Albert's home."

"Hard to tell when he's home," says Mother, "even when he's in."

Inside, the subject of Mother's snide remark shuffles to the stove where a pot of coffee perks on the gas burner.

"Thanks, darlin', smells good. Ya see who's come to visit?" Albert looks from Queenie to Mother without expression. "See how happy he is? Oh, we'll have great fun."

He moves to the counter where a tray bears three flowered

porcelain cups. The pot wobbles in his hand as he pours. Coffee trickles in a continuous flow to fill all three cups. The pot is replaced on the stove and the flame extinguished with deliberation. As Albert drifts past the sink he hooks the dishcloth without breaking his rhythm. The excess coffee in the tray is mopped and the bottom of the cups dried on his shirt tail. The obligation now discharged, he retreats to the living room.

"Thanks, darlin'," calls Queenie as he fades through the doorway.

"Albert Fong hasn't changed, has he?" says Mother a bit scornfully. "Still a fireball."

Queenie gives her a friendly push. "Now don't start. How was your trip? How'd ya break your wing? I gotta change. Be right back."

The air is sucked from the room as she departs and we lapse in the vacuum.

"How does your sister do it? Hockey at her age? I'm tired from just riding in the car." Even Albert Fong's coffee is stronger than I am.

"I dunno," says Mum, "but she's got her second wind."

"Gals! Gals! Come up and see my trophies," bawls Queenie from somewhere above us. "Bring the coffee with you."

"Always was a show off," sniffs Mother, "and don't think for a moment that hair's real."

Replacing the cups on the tray, I carry them upstairs to Queenie's bedroom, her non-stop patter a directional beacon.

The room is pink from rug to ruffled duvet fussing on the sleigh bed. Amid calendar pictures of butterball puppies pinned to the wall, are curling posters of Jacques Plante, the Gump, and Turk Broda loyally guarding their respective goals. One lonely sign of Albert Fong is an unused ashtray on one of the matching bedside tables.

Queenie, wrapped in a housecoat, launches into her presentation before a dresser topped with her awards.

"This is from the '87-'88 season. We kicked butt that year. This one," she continues, lofting a golden plastic model of a goalie, "is Most Valuable Player '88-'89." She flicks at the neighbouring one. "Next year we came second. The team that beat us was younger. Most of 'em weren't even collecting the pension. How's the coffee?" She plunges on without pause. "Now this one," a replica of the other two, "is for '91-'92 season. See, *Coolish Bearettes*. Stupid name but what can you do when the guys' team is the *Bears*. I wanted *Bearacuddas*, but I was a voice in the wilderness." Mother is about to interrupt but Queenie gives no ground. "Today is first practise for the new season. Ice was too soft but ..."

Mother calls a time-out, holding her hands up in a T. Queenie falls silent and Mum stick-handles into the hush. "We're happy for you. Aren't we happy for her, Edith?" Her voice rises in pitch. "But Queenie, dear, I've noticed the lack of festive embellishments," she circles her index finger in the air, "about the house. Is this because there IS no birthday party or because you choose to forget just how OLD you really are?"

"Unlike some people," says Queenie with a ruffling of feathers, "I'm proud to admit I'm sixty-five."

"Well, it makes me even prouder that you own up to it." To Mother's credit, she didn't taunt her further.

"You're still a snot-nose kid," Queenie fires. "Always were, always will be."

"Ladies, ladies," I try to restore order.

They circle each other like cats.

"Happy Birthday to-o-o you-u-u," I prompt. "Happy Birthday to-o-o- you-u-u." They retract their claws. "Happy Birthday, dear birthday girl." I ooze charm. "Happ ..."

"Alright, we get the picture," says Queenie. *We are not amused*.

"Kiss and make up then," I urge.

They hug briefly and buss the air near each other's cheeks. Mother has more colour in her face now and Queenie is a bit winded.

"The party, MY party," emphasises Queenie, "is tonight, six o'clock. You just made it in time. We've rented a hall."

"A hall," Mother archly informs me.

"Well, we started inviting a few people, then a few more, then others felt left out, and what can one do? The whole town, it seems, wants to be at my party."

"So, you got a hall?" Mum gnaws on this morsel.

"Ummm. And entertainment. And lots of food." Queenie picks up her discarded hockey uniform and deposits it into a pink laundry basket. "And our Wendy is going to be there with her fiancé."

Mother sees me roll my eyes and quickly changes the subject. "Is this affair dressy or what?"

"Wear what you have on," Queenie says, "no one will notice."

I grab Mum's fist as it rises and hold on. "I should bring in our suitcase and Mum's flowers. Where do we stay?"

The old rambling house is like a rabbit warren. At the furthermost end from her room, Queenie stops before two opposing doors. "I call them the blue room — that's yours Dix — and the brown room."

When ancient tombs are entered nowadays, the contained air is bottled and examined for mysteries of the past before the crypt is adulterated by modern visitors. The same should hold true here.

"Just open the window," Queenie instructs, pushing past us into the room. "Just needs freshening. I kept boarders for awhile but the excitement was too much for Albert."

I'm dithering outside the door of the brown room when Queenie crooks her finger in my direction. "Come. Come. Open a window and it'll be fine."

Dismantling the walls to let air in isn't going to rid the place of mothball smell. Queenie, noticing my recoil, clicks her tongue in annoyance. "Oh, Ardith, it's only temporary."

"Edith," I correct as I squat to lift the window. I can see the marble-like mothballs scattered under the iron bed. "Have a moth problem, do you?"

"Nope. They're to chase away raccoons. Had one climb the tree and make a nest in here. Helluva mess. Why d'ya think it's painted brown?" She rubs her eyes with the heel of her hands. "But that was after the old gentleman died."

"Now what old gentleman would that be?" I ask, not really wanting to know.

"One of the boarders we took in. Didn't show for supper when he was called, so Albert came up to check. Mr. Nistor died very neatly with his ankles crossed, hands behind his head. He'd stiffened like a board. They had a bit of a problem getting his elbows through the doorway." She illustrates by locking her hands behind her neck and stretching her elbows to touch the frame on either side. "Had to tilt him sideways."

"That's obscene," I state.

Mum's now keenly interested. She ducks under her sister's outstretched elbows to get in on the story. "Then what?"

"Albert went wild."

"Albert Fong?" says my sceptical Mother.

"Oh, Dix, you should have seen him." Queenie fans her face with her hand. "Pacing about on the lawn. He figured we'd never be able to rent the room again. And to top it all, he has this thing about boarders not showing up for a meal. Waste of good food."

I wedge myself into the conversation, "Let's back up here. An old man died in THIS room? This one here?"

"Oh, it was years ago. Don't worry about it. The sheets have been changed," she assures me before heading down the hall. "I'm almost positive they have."

▲

"What are you going to wear?" Mum asks, opening the suitcase on the blue chenille bedspread.

"I dunno," I answer. "Any old thing."

"What's the matter with you?" Mother says, sagging onto the bed.

"Nothing." I sulk, unwrapping the tissue paper crushed

around a purple suit. I wrote the copy for this one. Called it "classic silk for the Sears career woman. Softly gathered pants accent the slim figure. Dreamy blouse and opulent blazer complete the look. Comes in lily, jade or crushed grape." That's what it looks like now, crushed grape. "How am I going to get all the wrinkles out? And do you want to trade rooms?"

"Take it in the bathroom with you. Steam it out." She drags her two wearable outfits over her lap. "No trades," she says emphatically. "It's kinda like putting your underwear on inside out."

"I fail to see the connection."

"You're supposed to leave it inside out. To change it around means bad luck." Her index finger tacks the last two words in space. "Anyway, I don't want to sleep in that room."

"I hate to think it was somebody's death bed."

"Look on the bright side," she says pleasantly, "He's not still in it."

"You're all heart."

Queenie neglected to point it out, but I hope there's a bathroom behind one of the doors in the hallway.

I find it's the room next to mine — slope-ceilinged with an old-fashioned footed tub. The water has a beige tint, but it's hot. The wrinkles don't come out of me or the silk suit. Substantial amounts of makeup under my eye reduces the gangrenous look but the stitches' extended antennae above my eye look like curb feelers.

Mum thumps the door requesting water to wash down a couple of Tylenol. Wrapped in a towel, I carry the glass to her room. She backs onto the bed, clutching her cast.

"I can't even put nylons on," she complains.

"We don't have to go tonight, you know."

"Edith, after all the inconveniences we've been through just to get here, we're going to the party."

Inconveniences? Back in my dung-coloured room, switching the pillow to the foot of the bed and laying next to the open window allows me to follow the progress of cirro-cumulus clouds on their way to British Columbia.

A knock on the door and I call out, "Come in."

I expect Mum but instead a be-suited Albert Fong steps in, shifts his gaze away from me still in the towel and jabs at the face on his pocket watch. "Time," he says, replacing the watch in his vest pocket. I thank his retreating back.

Despite the fact that my comatose host is suffering a vested suit on this grand occasion, I forgo the wrinkled silk to wear a white jersey tee and oversize black and white checked shirt.

"You're not!" says Mother after I jostle her awake.

"These clothes are comfortable and they stay. Now, you want help or not?"

It's a squeeze to get her cast through the arm of her shirtdress, but I button her in. "But blue jeans?" she perseveres. "What if a man asks you to dance?"

"I'll tell him my mother won't let me 'cause I'm not wearing a skirt."

"Fine, Edith, make light of it. You want to look like a lumberjack, you'll hear no more from me."

That'll be the frosty Friday.

Albert's in the kitchen muttering as we descend the stairs.

"Here they are, Albert, quit fussing," Queenie snaps, handing him the car keys. "Go start the car, for Pete's sake." She addresses no one in particular. "Drives me crazy sometimes, playing with his earlobes while he waits." She pushes the chairs into the table then glances about the kitchen. "You'll have to take your own car, gals, 'cause we're picking up the Wackenbushes. Meet us at the hall."

"Where is the hall?" I ask, searching for my own keys.

"Down the road," Queenie waves vaguely. "Oh, by the way, Dix, you had a call."

"Why didn't you holler?"

"I figured you were sleeping."

"Who was it?" Mother asks.

"Oh, some man looking for his 'Mozzarella momma'." Queenie ushers us out the door. "Said you'd know who he was and that he'd be in touch."

"Walter," Mother says lyrically. She pursues her sister,

explaining, "That would be my Walter. You should'a come and got me. Maybe I should wait in case he calls again."

"I took care of it." Queenie stops so abruptly Mother runs into her. "You're not missing my birthday, so let's go."

"Did you tell him when we'd be back?"

"Hell, Dix, this could be a three-day affair."

"Like my Walter and me," says Mum wistfully.

"Life is full of surprises, ain't that so, Ardith?" Queenie winks broadly before nudging Albert out from behind the wheel.

"Edith. The name's EDITH!" I repeat dully. "Mother, how would you feel about going home?"

"Never mind, dear," she soothes, slipping her good arm around my waist. "She's always been the annoying one in the family. That's her way."

We load into our respective cars and Queenie pulls alongside, gunning the motor to keep it running. "Go back the way you came to reach the hall. Can't miss it."

"What's the place called?" I yell over the din.

"The Barrel ... ho-ou-s-s-se." The words languish in the car's dust as she floors it down the dirt road.

I turn to Mother for confirmation, "Did she say *Barrel-house*?"

"I do believe."

Funny how that makes me feel better.

Beneath a sign flashing GIRLS-GIRLS-GIRLS, an unlit billboard segregates patrons of the rental hall from those of the drinking establishment. FOnG PaRTY in irregular red plastic letters above an arrow points the way to a basement entrance.

A stage occupies one end of the lengthy room while the other holds a kitchen behind folding doors. Long tables at right angles to the food counter are set to receive the bounty of a potluck dinner. Pink and white streamers twist from the rafters. Matching plastic roses bloom in waterless vases.

"Do we sit anywhere?" I wonder aloud, eyeing the chairs aligned with regularity. "Reminds me of a school banquet. Dance to follow."

"Do you think we should have stopped for a can of something as an offering?" asks Mother, as women bearing quilt-wrapped casseroles veer directly to the kitchen. Gift boxes lashed with ribbon are stowed on a card table.

"Your half-jar of ginger is still rolling around the trunk," I remind her.

"No bloody way," she states, pulling me into a chair next to her. "That jar's mine."

As the room fills with much of Coolish's population, the kids dive under the tables or run circles around each other in the middle. Resentful teens loll with their backs against the wall, longing to be elsewhere.

The Wackenbushes and the Albert Fongs arrive, Queenie pausing to make a grand entrance. She sweeps in to acknowledge a smattering of applause that underscores a chorus of "Happy Birthdays", taking her place regally on a folding chair. Helium balloons tied to the back dip and bob over her head. She sits, knees together, offering a three-fingered handshake to well-wishers while Albert, her consort, returns outside to smoke, ardently inhaling as much as his lungs allow. He's not included in the group of self-conscious men in ill-fitting suits, hoisting ten-year-old shoes onto rusting truck bumpers.

Inside, the women sweat within the humid kitchen, arranging fried chicken, beef stew and garden vegetables in different areas of the warming ovens. Deep-dish apple, Saskatoon and rhubarb pies invite a coronary within their flaky lard-based pastry. Cabbage rolls, coleslaw enough to fill a child's wading pool, pickled crabapples and garlic dills cover the banquet table. Thick blue china plates are stacked on chairs so as not to take up the assigned space for the fragrant mountain of fresh rolls.

"Bet they've never heard of cottage cheese and fruit salad." Mum nods, but I don't think she's really listening.

After one of the kitchen helpers waves like she's flagging down a train, Queenie rises, clapping her hands.

"Friends," she calls out unheeded. "Friends and neighbours!" It makes no inroad to the cannonade of chatter. Queenie raises the same three fingers used for her handshake, holds the middle one down with her thumb, sticks the tips of the other two into her mouth and blows. There's immediate silence as the last of the screaming whistle ricochets around the room. "Friends and neighbours," she summons, "it's time to eat."

Children who can't wait for plates queue first, pushing ahead to snatch up the drumsticks. They are scolded back to the fold.

I volunteer to fetch Mother's dinner and while I wait in line, a bear of a man stands too close behind, breathing on my neck. To discourage him I step back, trying for his toes but tromping on steel-reinforced boots. I think he takes it as foreplay.

"Ya new in town?" he rumbles. "Ain't seen you b'fore."

Using my elbow as a persuader, I half turn to answer. It moves him not an inch. "We're just visiting."

"Who," he says in a garlicky gust, "ya visitin'?"

"Queenie Fong." Now that I've reached the head of the line, I move along two steps, arranging a variety of home cooking onto our plates.

He stays sucked-up behind, topping his mound of food with a rivulet of ketchup. "That Queenie's a good goalie. Doesn't flop," he says, nodding in agreement with his own opinion. "Where ya sittin' at?" He holds his fork like a weapon. I pretend not to hear. He bumps me with his ample belly. "Where ya sittin' at?"

"Over there," I mumble, thankful that Mother is saving the only chair between her and a ten year-old with a red bow tie.

When I fail to live up to his expectations, the bear's big head sweeps left and right looking for other game. "I'll save ya a spot on my dance card," he promises benevolently.

▲

There's nothing left on my plate but the colour and I lean against Mum confessing, "I don't think I can walk, I ate so much."

"Maybe, dear heart, one piece of pie would have sufficed."

"Now you tell me," I groan.

Queenie walks to mid-floor, swishing her blue and silver skirt. Albert trails behind fingering his earlobe, looking uncomfortable in the shared limelight. She gives another whistle, short and sharp.

"Friends and neighbours," she announces without benefit of microphone, "Albert and I thank you for the wonderful turnout. It's not everyday a girl turns twenty-nine." She waits for the predictable response. "While the washers-up clear the dishes, we'll play a few games for prizes." She prods Albert to hand over the brown shopping bag he carries on his arm. "It's going to be just like *The Price Is Right*," she claims, holding the sack as if it contains crown jewels.

"We can go now if you like," I say optimistically, "before we have to do tricks."

Mother ignores me.

Albert Fong casts a longing look over his shoulder to the exit door, then taps his breast pocket to make sure his cigarettes are still there.

"I think we'll start," says Queenie, looking pointedly in our direction, "with a prize for the person who travelled the farthest to be here on such a special occasion."

"Awww, no," I wince. "I'm telling you, Mother, I'm not,

repeat not, going up there."

"That person is my dear sister, Dixie Flood, who's dragged herself all the way over the mountains from Vancouver. As you can see she's suffered an injury." Queenie looks suitably empathetic. "And with her is her daughter ... Audra."

That's the last straw. I bolt to my feet, "IT'S EDITH, GODDAMMIT! E-D-I-T-H. EDITH." I have everyone's attention.

Mother shades her eyes.

"Thank you for sharing that with us," Queenie remarks with sugar-coated rancour. "Now if Dixie will come and get her little gift from Albert, we'll carry on."

"Speaking of carrying on ..." Mum expounds, knocking me with her casted arm before pitter-pattering toward Queenie. Albert Fong pushes a rumpled package into his wife's hand and steps back three paces.

"Come, E-E-DITH," Queenie enunciates, "we want everybody to meet you, too."

I half rise and give a peace sign. Jeez, I feel stupid. I haven't flashed those two particular fingers together since the '60s.

"Right on," says the kid in the red bow tie.

Queenie persists, "She's turned shy, folks. Let's give her a Coolish welcome." Applause and stomping ring the room like the wave at a hockey game. Albert, backing up at a snail's pace so as not to draw notice, is now halfway to the door.

I slouch, planting one foot before the other to reach the mid-room festivities, two long miles away. I'd rather leave with Albert Fong.

"So lovely to have family at a time like this." Queenie throws her arm around Mother, then includes me in the hug long enough to pinch skin between finger and thumb. It seems to be a family trait. "May look like these two were on the losing end of a train wreck, folks," — a spirited whistling and stomping accompanies Queenie's gesture as she hoists Mother's plaster cast — "but they had a little car accident in Indian Head. We're happy to say they're on the mend." Mother gives a curtsy and reclaims her arm, holding it against her waist. Queenie, enjoying the spotlight, continues. "I'll just tell all you eligible men out there that these two are single and available."

Damned if that heavy-breathing bear of a man doesn't slap his knee in delight.

Queenie dismisses us with a wave, then toils on. "A prize as well to our lovely daughter Wendy, who bussed in from Yorkton to be with us." Queenie reaches into her bag for another gift as Wendy and her male companion abandon their table. "And Wendy's fiancé of ... How long's it been, Phred?"

Phred, grinning, turns with his arms straight up, nine fingers in the air, so all can see.

Albert Fong, his future father-in-law, casts a doleful look at the assembly, then quietly shuts the exit door behind him.

"... as I was saying, Wendy's intended of nine long years, Phred Applegate." Phred tilts to whisper in Queenie's ear. "Says I'm to remind you he's in the cleaning business."

"Vacuums, new and used," he advertises. "Anytime you're in Yorkton."

Wendy and her Mother confer, then urge Phred to return to his seat. Wendy's hand gesture promises removal of his heart with a spoon if he doesn't comply. Knowing when to retreat seems to be another of Phred's finer qualities. Earlier, Queenie, buffing up his image to impress us, had mentioned the other two qualities — his being single and his generous dental plan.

Wendy hefts her mother's proffered gift suspiciously. The box is ticking audibly and the shaking Wendy gives it sets off a tinny alarm within. Her cheeks spot with high colour as she gives her mother a venomous glare.

"What's that all about?"

"I think mother just gave daughter a not-so-subtle hint."

"I don't get it," I say, watching Wendy move clumsily back to her table.

"Engaged nine years? Her biological clock tick, tick, ticking away."

"Poor Weeny." A meddling mother, a reluctant suitor and

a serious overbite is more than I could have wished for. As a kid, Wendy did hateful things when we were forced by circumstance into each other's company. She inflated frogs with a straw and once blamed me for setting fire to a woodshed but she was the one inside igniting the sparks of some hormonal male. She once even tried, unsuccessfully, to get Verna to eat dog poop on the end of a stick. When Verna and I were old enough to rebel at having her visit for summer holidays we lost touch.

Mum puts down her water glass. "Unmarried daughters are a worry."

"Don't you start," I threaten. She widens her eyes all innocent-like.

"Now," says Queenie, still holding court, "if the men will fold up the tables and the ladies move the chairs back, we'll get on with the dance."

Amid the clatter of locking metal legs being kicked and folded under the trestle tables, the stage at the end of the hall is graced with a stool and a microphone. Next out is a large dusty areca palm which is tipped off the dolly and rolled next to the stool. This potted foliage, stamped *property of the Barrelhouse Bar*, completes the stage decorations.

"Mum, it's ten to eight. Let's go."

"Not before the dance."

"You gonna dance with a cast on your arm?"

"I know what you're doing, Edith. Don't impose your anti-socialness onto me," she says, heatedly. "I love dancing."

"But ..."

"No buts. You don't like dancing, go hide in a corner."

"I'll help in the kitchen then." I flounce to the back of the hall but they flap me out with their aprons.

There really isn't a dark enough or remote enough corner to bury myself in. *If I just sit here and look miserable, nobody will ask me to dance. Maybe I should pull out my stitches and bleed a little. That would be a sure-fire deterrent.* I'll go upstairs to GIRLS-GIRLS-GIRLS and search out Denis. As I head for the doorway the microphone whistles and the effervescent Queenie surfaces yet again.

"We promised entertainment and here it is," she announces, struggling to hoist herself onto the stool. Failing that, she lifts the mike from the stand instead. "Live from Vancouver, Calgary, Edmonton, everywhere ... THE POLKA-A-A CZARS."

She looks stage right then cups her ear. "Huh?" She sidesteps, tipping toward the wings, "Whad'ya say?"

More sidesteps, "WH-A-A-T?"

Queenie suddenly charges, trailing wires.

"WHAT D'YA MEAN NO POLKA CZARS?"

Her amplified voice swells over the dying applause, reaching Tizzie, the bar owner above, who realizes Queenie isn't taking the cancellation news well. He scrambles for his car keys. Her voice carries to the serious drinkers at the bar whose eyes clear briefly. It pierces the concentration of the exotic dancer who for the first time ever, fumbles her ping pong balls. Albert, believing the voice to be akin to God's, returns to the hall and his place at the birthday table.

Queenie, taking her goalie stance, demands the identity of the offstage personality. "WHO THE HELL ARE YOU?" she calls. "WHO?" She stares unbelieving at the business card she is handed. "And just *who* cancelled the Polka Czars?"

Even old Mrs. Wackenbush rises unaided, hand fumbling with the controls of her hearing aid, not wanting to miss a word.

"I'LL KILL HIM, THE LITTLE WEASEL." Every eye is on the hostess as she stomps mid-stage. After adjusting a piece of lingerie that has dared to go against her, she begins a silent count of ten, then slowly speaks, "Friends ... and ... neighbours. I am sorry to inform you ..." her voice breaks, "TIZZIE WILL PAY FOR THIS." She recovers from her momentary lapse. "Ya see, folks, we arranged for the Polka Czars. Didn't we, Albert?" He nods like one of those animated dogs placed in the back window of cars. "The Polka Czars were cancelled." A sigh of aw-w-ws reaches Queenie. "It's okay, friends," she sympathizes, "we're here for a good time and that's what we're gonna have. Right?" It's a ragtag

THE CADILLAC KIND

answer. "RIGHT?" she repeats. When the chorus dies, she continues, "... as I was saying, DI-rect from Indian Head ..." She checks the small white card she has palmed.

Couldn't be. I release the door and come back inside.

"A man known in his own mind as Mr. Excitement ... DINKMEISTER." Laughter greets her introduction. "Huh?" Queenie consults with Mr. Excitement. "Sorry, people, it's Dink (pause) Meister." She returns the microphone to the stand and urges him onstage and to move with greater haste.

With his usual enthusiasm Denis ambles across the stage, laying his guitar flat on the stool before acknowledging the tepid welcome. He returns to the wings to retrieve his accordion case which he opens near the potted palm. A fresh round of applause, even a few whistles, greets this action.

I'll stay but I won't dance.

Denis tosses his ponytail and lifts the instrument into position. He looks out at the convention with those unconventional eyes until the crowd quiets.

The quiet becomes awkward.

He runs his fingers over the buttons, then lowers his head and explodes with ... "The Beerbarrel Polka".

Atta boy, Denis. Give 'em hell.

Heads nod in approval as the floor clears for the dancers. Queenie, leaning heavily on the banister leading down the stage steps, looks drawn beneath her new-penny hair colour. She addresses the glad-handing of friends with appreciation as she doe-see-doe's her way to Albert Fong. He gives her a kiss on the forehead.

A gasp of garlic curls past my ear. I hear him breathing. The bear wants to dance.

"Sorry, I can't. My leg," I say, grabbing at it. "Injured in the accident. I'll never polka again."

"Ya can sue for that, ya know." He removes his baseball cap long enough to scratch his head. A dusting of dry scalp falls into his eyebrows and onto his humpy shoulders.

"That's being considered," I tell him.

"Ya know, I use good old horse liniment on mysel' when I stiffen up."

Spare the thought.

"Got some in the pick-up. Wanna come out and I'll rub yer leg?"

"What's your name?" I ask, wondering if he knew the answer.

"Bob."

"Well, Bob, that might be the best offer I'll get all day, but no."

"No polka. No liniment. Are you tryin' to tell me somethin'?"

"Is that in the realm of possibility?" I say, gracing the remark with a smile.

He looks befuddled as if he's treed the wrong quarry. "Maybe a waltz?"

"Sure, Bob. I could probably manage a waltz." *All you have to do is find me.* "Will you excuse me, please." I feel the polka may be coming to an end.

I make it as far as the door, dragging my poor crippled leg, when Mr. Entertainment's tempo slows to the Beerbarrel *Waltz*. I look to see how much distance I've put between Bob and me.

About eight inches.

From the rotundity parting the green workshirt, a rumbling request, "May I have this dance?" He replaces the hat. Nose hair grows uncropped.

"Uh-h-h-h-h, I was just …" I falter.

He holds up his right paw in a ten o'clock position and the left at four. His boots start a shuffle and the bear head nods almost in time to the beat.

"I …"

He takes my hand, placing it on his shoulder. The impact sends up a flurry of dandruff. My other hand is trapped within his. "One and two, and one and two." He looks at his feet, marking time.

With his counting, I don't have to carry on a conversation. One small blessing.

When Denis finally runs out of steam, I make a break. Bob, good old bear, stays by my side. I search the room for a rescuer. Mother is sitting where I left her but she seems somehow different. She's taller and has her arms wrapped around a beachball. "Must go, Bob. Mother calls."

For someone with a bad leg, I make good time across the room. Darting between people, I hear Mother's laugh over the general commotion. She must be into the home-brew I see circulating. A glimpse in her direction shows her sitting sideways in her chair, but there are two plump trousered legs beneath her, facing forward. Below those well-pressed pants are wing-tip shoes.

The "beachball" she is clutching to her bosom has glasses, and magnified behind those glasses are half-closed contented eyes. And in the hand that isn't stroking my mother is a stump of dead cigar. She's sitting on Walter's lap! And he's nuzzling her ear. Damn. If I hadn't been with that performing bear I could have nailed him at the door. Maybe Bob was a setup, like Verna and brother-in-law Bernard. No doubt, Bob-the-bear and Walter will give each other a high-five later when they pass.

"Walter? How nice," I lie.

"Hel-lo, Edith," he says jovially. *At least HE remembers my name.* "You girls have had quite a trip. Dixie here has been an inspiration, hasn't she?"

Dixie here is beaming, her gold tooth reflecting in Walter's spectacles. He coos and murmurs into her neck. I take a seat, trying to ignore the two of them. In a few moments Mother tells him "she is firsty," and he answers this foolishness with more of his own: "What would my dumpling like?" After their puckish giggles are over, he waddles away to the refreshment table. I am left to wonder at his devotion. Should I tell him she has no money?

She sighs, "Isn't it exciting? Walter right here in Coolish!"

"Why is he here? It's a long way from home."

"He missed his little pudding," she says coyly.

"Don't you think his pudding is being a bit hasty?"

"Are we being bitchy, Toots?" She searches him out through the crowd. "He's worried about me, the accident and all. Says he doesn't want to lose a good thing."

"Good thing, Mother, or SURE thing?"

She wiggles her fingers at him as he approaches, but says from the side of her mouth, "Shut your face, dearie."

"Here you go, ladies. I brought you one, too, Edith." He bumps into Mum's arm in passing. "Sorry, my angel," he apologises, kissing the fingers of the limp little hand extending from the plaster. "I wouldn't hurt you for anything."

She shoots me a triumphant look over his bowed head. A look that says I'll be eating crow.

Denis detonates another polka and the party-goers rise to the challenge. Bob-the-bear has found another partner — a large red-faced woman, finally out of the kitchen, who charges him through the dance. He looks shell-shocked. His cap is lost in the robust gallop.

When it's over, Denis taps the microphone for attention. "Today is the sixty-fifth birthday of a very special lady. Can we clear the floor for Queenie Fong and her husband ..." he checks the writing on his open palm, "... Albert. I'll play them a little something I threw together called 'Climbing the Waltz'." He plays a few notes while people form a loose circle around Queenie and Albert. "I'm told we'll have the cake at intermission and wish this lovely lady a Happy Birthday." He wipes his forehead on his sleeve and adds, "And maybe a guy can get a cold one?"

Before he can begin in earnest, a lithe young thing steps fawn-like across the stage to hand him a Coke. *I don't believe that's what he had in mind.* She gazes while he drinks, then catches herself and hurries off, self-consciously.

Queenie and Albert join hands and begin the dance. Her blue and silver skirt circles above his patent leather shoes as she pirouettes beneath his raised arm, then they drift as one across the wooden floor. Albert Fong lives!

"Wow, do you see that?" I say to Mum waiting hand-in-hand with Walter.

She gives me a funny look. "Don't you remember?"

"Remember what?"

"Where Albert and Queenie met?" When I shake my head

she tells me. "Before he was a barber he was an Arthur Murray dance instructor. Cha cha, rumba, tango, you name it. She showed us her hockey trophies but she has even more for their ballroom dancing. He's the best." She quickly checks to see if Walter's offended. "After you, of course," she adds.

He gives her hand a squeeze, then looks up at me. "Would you mind if your mother and I dance?" Mother rises eagerly. "One moment, Dixie." He waits for my answer.

"Certainly, Walter," I say, like a pontifical blessing. *I resist making the sign of the cross. Domini. Domini.*

As other couples also begin to take the floor, Mother releases Walter's hand to confide to me in a stage whisper, "Walter and I are going for a drive after this. A little trip. Don't wait up."

"Then you don't need a ride home?"

"That's right."

He leads her into the music and they gaze into each other's eyes as they bump along. They are not Queenie and Albert.

The bear is leaning, forehead to the wall by the bathrooms, his hat stuffed into his back pocket. The large red-faced woman is patting his shoulder in consolation. Three teenage girls, fresh as new bread, wait for Denis to finish.

"Guess I'll just go home," I say to my purse. "Should've done it hours ago."

The music trails out the door as it closes behind me. Here in the parking lot is where some of the men are hanging out. Bottles in brown bags, roll-your-own cigarettes. Walter's motorhome rises like a moon above the half-tons.

I drive home alone but it's not until pulling up in front of Queenie's house that I remember I don't have a key. But this is Coolish. A cat sleeping on the stoop slinks away as I approach. The door opens at a push and I enter the darkened house. Mother's hospital flowers now emit a cloying stink.

After washing up, I gladly put on my long ratty nightgown. A good sleep should take away my headache. I wearily roll into Mother's bed and curl under the blue chenille spread. What the hell, she's not going to use it tonight. The ceiling reflects car headlights driving the country road.

Sometime during the next few hours I hear Queenie arrive home, reliving the evening. Albert Fong is probably nodding his head at anything requiring a response.

In that black velvet darkness, Walter's motorhome is likely testing out that stupid two-dollar bumper sticker ... If this motorhome's a-rockin' ... Naw, not at their age.

After Albert Fong and Queenie settle in, I sleep fitfully until 6:30, then birdsongs and the smell of fresh coffee lure me out.

I'm surprised to see a lone figure at the table.

"'Morning, Uncle Albert. Coffee smells wonderful." Two thick rimmed mugs sit on the same tray that yesterday held porcelain teacups. "Queenie still sleeping?"

He nods once, hunching over his cup as if it were the last source of heat. The coffee has a lot of body. A good kickstart to the day.

"So," I say, making conversation, "how did you like the party? Loved your waltzing."

He bobs his head.

"Denis, the musician from last night, is a friend from Indian Head. We gave him a ride to Coolish."

"Needs a haircut," says Albert Fong, scraping back his chair.

"That's the style nowadays."

"Sold her just in time then." He clips his words neatly as a short-back-and-sides.

"Sold what?" I ask as he pours another coffee.

Albert Fong shakes loose a cigarette before answering, "Barbershop." He leans over the counter to gaze out the window, turning his back on any more chatter.

I carry my cup through the living room to the front stoop. The same cat that darted away in the night now crouches in the sunshine across the body of a plump gopher, its legs trying to escape the cat's jaws.

"Here kitty. Nice kitty," I coax, attempting a rescue. The cat growls and teeters away, the gopher dragging between its front legs. "Stupid cat." I look for a rock to throw. It's only when I'm away from the door that I see the motorhome parked under the overhanging willow, not fifty feet from my car. She's back.

"YOOOOOOO HOOOOOOO, sweetheart," Mother yodels as she spots me from its open door.

I drop the rock.

"Edith, come he-e-e-y-e-r-r." She beckons exaggeratedly. "Walter has made so-o-o much breakfast we'll need help."

He appears behind her dressed in an apron and not much else. He waves the bacon tongs repeating her gestures. "Coffee's on," he calls, then turns back inside to his cooking duties. He's not actually as nude as he looks, for he's wearing peach shorts and a matching muscle shirt. Both Walter and Mother withdraw inside.

I roll down the car windows in passing as it promises to be another warm day, then lean against the motorhome waiting to be urged in. Begged in. Walter comes to the door with a plate of sizzling bacon, hash browns and two eggs over easy. Coronary-to-go.

"Toast and crumpets inside," he lures.

That comes close enough to begging to count.

Once we all slide around Walter's tidal-pool table, the air-conditioned atmosphere is quite genial. Without any prodding they tell me about the rest of last night's party. Apparently, Mother and Walter were having such a lovely time they didn't leave on their little trip as planned. Queenie insisted they stay.

"Old Albert doesn't say much but he's a good listener. Real interested in the cheese biz."

"And your young man had the lights dimmed when the birthday cake came in so we could all sing 'Happy Birthday'. Queenie staged a few tears." Mum dabs at her eyes to illustrate the story.

"Which 'young man' is mine?" I ask.

"Oh, come off it, Edith. Denis, of course. He looked for you, once he found out we were all at the same affair. Just never tied us up with the name Fong. Please pass the toast, sweetie." And sweetie does, with puppy eyes. "He even played a song for you."

"Yeah, right."

"Am I lying, Walter?" Walter obediently shakes his head. "See?" she says obstinately.

"Well, that's too bad because he's going back to Indian Head today on the bus." I clean my plate with the last bit of crumpet and Walter pours more coffee from an insulated jug. "Which reminds me, Mother, how long are we staying?"

The roar of silence is broken by Walter clearing his throat. They have a quick visual consultation across the table. "Ummm, Edith?" says Mother tentatively. Walter's expansive forehead furrows.

I set the cup down, waiting for the shoe to drop.

"Walter and I ..."

"Your mother and I ..." he smiles indulgently.

"Dixie, you first." He unties his apron and hangs it inside a cupboard.

"It's this way." Mother stiffens her resolve. "Walter and I want to go on from here and see the rest of Canada and maybe take a swing through the States on our way back home." And she doesn't even add "if it's alright with you, dear."

But Walter does. He slides in beside me, his plump fingers grasping the hand I've carelessly left lying around. "This means you'll have the drive back all by yourself ... unless you'd like to travel with us?"

"She has to go back to work, Walter. Don't you?" She shoots me that warning look. "Dear."

"It doesn't happen often, Walter, but she's right. I really should be heading back." I draw my hand out from under his. "Spent my holidays in a motel in Indian Head waiting for her to get out of hospital."

"And time well spent it was, Edith. She's certainly worth waiting for." He blows her a kiss.

"I'm outnumbered here. You two have a great time. Thanks for asking, Walter, but me, I'm leaving within the hour." I return to the house.

Albert Fong is back in his appointed place, the barber

chair, crossword book open on his knee. Queenie is at the table, her electric hair in rollers.

"'Morning," I say as I pass her chair. "I'll be upstairs packing."

She's fast on her feet, right behind me as I reach the bedroom. "What's going on? How come you two are leaving already? Your Mother still parked outside with that little cheese man?" Her economy of cramming three questions into one breath is a wonder.

"'Fraid so. They'll be tripping across the country together, in the opposite direction to me. I'm heading to Vancouver. Alone." I sit on the side of the bed, my legs straight out before me, feeling forlorn.

"Poor baby," she says, which is just the right thing to say. "My sister's still unreasonable, I see. They spoiled her and she hasn't changed."

"S'okay. I'll probably enjoy myself. No beer parlour brawls, no backtalk."

"Told us last night about being held hostage. The woman's a wacko, you know. She could'a died." Queenie paces in her agitation.

"Wacko's a little strong." Not much of a defense.

"Anyway, Ardith, when you going? I got a hockey practise this morning." She spots a cobweb hanging from the ceiling and waves it away. "Wanna come and watch?"

"Thanks, but I'm leaving as soon as I pack all this stuff." I throw the suitcase on the bed. "Tell Mother her clothes are here." I pile her things to one side.

"Tell her yourself." She stands and stretches, not quite ready to leave alone the subject of Mother. "That little man dotes on her. God knows why." Queenie paces, the wooden floor squeaking underfoot. "I think it's an act of desperation."

I'm absorbed in finding the exact board that makes the noise but Queenie stops moving.

"No fist fights on the premises, okay?" She raps my head with her knuckles before she thumps out the door and down the hall, leaving me to the packing.

After flinging the suitcase into the trunk of the car, I see

Queenie in her hockey uniform pushing Albert Fong into their doorway to wave goodbye. Walter and Mother are in his doorway. It's like an old tintype in sepia colours: the doorways barred by unsmiling couples. Nothing moves in that second but time itself. As the cat drags another gopher toward the stoop the moment ends.

"Bye, Edith," calls Queenie. *She finally got my name right.* "Thanks for the canning." Albert Fong returns inside.

Mother, urged on by Walter, walks to the car with the plaster cast supported on her hip. Her face looks like a storm warning.

"What?" I ask abruptly, leaning against the fender.

"Don't," she warns, "be mad at Walter."

"I'm not." She keeps her distance, blowing her nose on a Kleenex fished from her pocket.

"You're mad at me, then?" she asks flatly, looking down at her only pair of shoes powdered with Manitoba dust.

"Goddam right," I say, "I'm mad at you." So what if she cries. "Even at forty-two I feel abandoned by you. Like I'll do for company until something better comes along."

"I'm only gonna say this once, Toots. You ARE the best thing to come along." She reaches her arms around my neck. The cast thumps my back. "I'm happy you're my daughter." She kisses my neck before pulling away.

Maybe she's not so bad. "Me, too." I climb into the car and close the door.

"You look after that eye. Get the stitches out," she says, "then you won't look so bad."

"There's egg yolk on your chin."

"No!" she says, unbelieving. She cranks the side-view mirror to see, then spits on the Kleenex and wipes away the yellow dribble, stepping back as the car starts.

At the house, Queenie waves one last time then joins Albert Fong inside. Walter sits at his table holding the curtain aside to watch the departure.

"Gotta go, Mum."

She grasps the car door looking like she wants to say something. Maybe a few sacrosanct words to live by. Words passed through the generations from mother to daughter.

She plants two kisses on my face. "Grab a life, sweetheart."

That's it? My oracle. "Grab a life, sweetheart"? Her words of wisdom don't even come with a chunk of free cheese.

A curling plume of dust behind the car soon obscures her. She disappears into the Manitoba morning. Like Oz. The side-view mirror with its rakish tilt reflects turquoise sky.

I linger too long at the stop sign which precipitates an impatient beep behind me. Instead of flashing the finger, I leave my car and approach the other driver.

"Can you tell me where the bus depot is in Coolish?"

"Let's see," she says, squinting toward the town in the distance. "I believe it's next to the café."

As if it will help me to distinguish the buildings, I also gaze toward Coolish. "Which café?"

"There's only one. You can't miss it." She taps her gas pedal in anticipation.

"Thanks." When I'm back in the car I signal her to go around. I need a moment more to think this out.

Coolish is T-shaped, with the top of the T being the main street running east and west. The stem of the T extends south for a short determined stretch before meandering off into brown grassland.

She's right, I couldn't miss it. Before the Lone Wolf Café, the west-bound Greyhound waits with its side flaps open ingesting mouldering suitcases and twine-tied brown boxes. I park far enough away to scan the passengers without being noticed myself. I feel as breathless as if I'd run all the way here. Must be all the breakfast I put away. Travellers hold tickets out to the indifferent driver as he bars entrance to the bus.

There's no guitar case being hugged by an aspiring musician in gold chains. No battered accordion case. I wait until the bus is loaded and the doors close before deserting my post. Damn. I was looking forward to the company.

The bus exhausts a sigh of blue as the driver puts the thing into gear. He waits for me to pass before lumbering away from the curb.

I try the radio. It's silent until I reach over and kick the underside repeatedly. The discharge of static is suddenly interrupted by music, sweet and clear. Connie Kaldor's "Wood River". Things are looking up. Radio's working, emergency brake is working. All I have now is another ten thousand miles to go.

"Wood River" fades when electrical interference closes in. More kicking does not bring about more music. I switch it off, vowing to replace it. Someday. Maybe if desperation sets in by Indian Head, I'll take it to Vonnie. In the meantime, I'll hum.

I pass the Barrelhouse, then slow down and double back to circle the parking lot. *Just in case.* The only thing there at that time of morning is a truck with a flat rear tire. As I wait to get back onto the highway, the Greyhound passes by heading west. I follow the tail lights until he signals a right turn. Ahead on the horizon in front of a rundown motel, a lone passenger flags down the bus. I'm about to pass when something familiar makes me hang back. The bus shudders to a stop in front of a lean figure shouldering a guitar case. Between his feet a backpack and another piece of baggage too big for a carry-on.

I sound the horn as the driver opens the luggage compartment. He looks up, annoyed at the effrontery. Denis gives me a long look and I know I'm making a terrible mistake. Mother tells me to get a life and here I am being rash and impulsive. I'll just back up and drive away. No one will be the wiser.

Denis speaks briefly to the driver as he is about to stow the accordion. The driver tilts his hat back and stands, hands on hips, watching his passenger walk away.

"Want a lift, fella?"

"I dunno. Ma told me never to accept rides from strange people."

There's a sound of crunching gravel as the bus pulls away.

"You're safe," I assure him, "I left all the strange people in Coolish."

"Speaking of which, where's your mother?" He's leaning

against the car trying to adjust the side-view mirror from its cockeyed angle.

"Get in and I'll tell you."

He loads his stuff into the back seat then reaches to the floor. "You taking home a souvenir?"

"What do you mean?" I turn to see what he has.

He holds the stiff bodies of two gophers over the front seat. "They're great toasted over an open fire." *Damn cat.*

I cover my head and duck away.

"You could open a drive-in and call it McGopher's. A whole new career." He chucks them into the adjacent field before climbing into the passenger side.

"No more back there?"

"Naw, just the pair," he says. "So ... what's happening?"

"I'm heading home, that's all."

"All by yourself, huh? That because of your mother's boyfriend?" he teases.

"You met him?"

"Do you know Italians like their mozzarella made from water-buffalo milk? Or that Cheshire cheese is saltier than cheddar because those damn cows graze on Cheshire's salty plains?"

"You met him," I nod knowingly.

"Oh yeah! Last night. And where were you while I entertained the troops?"

"Once everybody paired off, I went home. It gave me an excuse to leave."

"And your Mother is ... ?"

"About to venture east in a motorhome. She and the crown prince of cheese will be on tour."

"And how do you feel about that?" he asks.

"It's her life."

"No, no, Edith," he persists, digging, digging. "I asked how you FEEL about that. In your gut."

"Hey, I'm fine. Okay?" *None of his bloody business.*

"That's bullshit!"

A flush of anger prickles my face. "You want to know how I goddam feel?" I say heatedly, pulling to the side of the

Trans-Canada. "Then I'll goddam tell you." I rush to take a breath. "Accidentally ran over something on the road one day." As if he's in for a long testimony, Denis stretches out, crossing his long legs at the ankle. "I went back to see and found a snake. It wasn't dead but a bit of tail was squashed into the road. The poor thing tried desperately to get away but this little mangled piece held him back."

Denis chews his thumb nail as he waits for me to continue.

I sit, arms crossed, expecting a reaction.

"Yeah?" he urges.

"Well, that's me!" I reveal, thumping my index finger on my chest. "MY tail stuck to the road, waiting for the next set of wheels." I jiggle the gearshift.

"Hold on," he says, looking bemused. "What happened to the snake?"

"Scraped him off the road with a stick," I shrug. "He disappeared into the grass."

"So he lives to fight another day?"

I put the car into gear. "Guess so."

"Enough said."

He reaches back for his guitar and chords awhile, leaving me alone with my thoughts.

When I'm through feeling sorry for myself I make a musical request. "Can you play any Willie Nelson songs?"

"Name it," he boasts. "Anything at all, I can play." He breaks into a fiery flamenco.

"'Golden Earrings'."

"Never heard of it. You made it up," he challenges.

"Did not!" I argue. "It's Willie's song and you don't know it? Thought you knew everything."

"How 'bout 'Sunny Side of the Street'? 'On the Road Again'?" he asks, chording the latter.

"Nope, only 'Golden Earrings'. Too bad 'cause I'm a big tipper."

"Edith?"

"Uh huh."

"When do you have to be back at work?"

"Why?"

"I have a plan," he says, smiling at me with those funny eyes.

"What would that be?"

"You answer first."

"I have another week. And … ?"

"Seeing as I threw away the gophers, can we stop up ahead for coffee and subs? I'll tell you then." He's playing coy. No hints, just a look about him.

I give him the once-over as he carries the food back to the car. God, he looks good in jeans.

"Okay, tell me your plan," I say, when we're nearly finished eating.

"How would you … ?" he begins. "Naw, wouldn't work. Forget it."

"What? What wouldn't work?" I bite.

"It's too crazy. You're a busy person." He shakes his head solemnly.

"Damn it, you're annoying."

"How about … going to Duck Lake to see Joe Fafard?"

"Wha-a-a-t?"

"Sure, wouldn't take long. He's still there."

"I thought you had the court case?"

"I do, this afternoon. We could start first thing in the morning."

"Let me think about it."

"No hurry," he says, looking at his watch. "Time's up. Wanna go?"

"Well," I say tentatively, "okay."

"That's it?" he yells, "just … okay?" He drawls "okay" like a 78-record played on slow speed.

I jump from the car leaving the door open and find a patch of grass big enough for what I have in mind. Back … back … then make a run, tossing myself into a pretty good cartwheel. It goes so surprisingly well I throw caution to the wind and do another.

"OKAY!"

Thank you to the god of cartwheels for not letting me make a bigger fool of myself. After I pick up the loose pocket change I return to the car.

"Will that suffice?" I ask, self-satisfied.

He reaches for his guitar as I pull onto the highway.

· THE POLESTAR FIRST FICTION SERIES ·

The Polestar First Fiction series celebrates the first published book of fiction — short stories or novel — of a Canadian writer. Polestar is committed to supporting new writers, and contributing to North America's dynamic and diverse cultural fabric.

Polestar Book Publishers takes pride in creating books that enrich our understanding and enjoyment of the world, and in introducing discriminating readers to exciting new writers. Whether in prose or poetry, these independent voices illuminate our history, stretch our imaginations, engage our sympathies and evoke the universal through narrations of everyday life.

Polestar titles are available from your local bookseller. For a copy of our complete catalogue — featuring poetry, fiction, fiction for young readers, sports books and provocative non-fiction — please contact us at:

POLESTAR BOOK PUBLISHERS
1011 Commercial Drive, Second Floor
Vancouver, British Columbia
CANADA   V5L 3X1
phone (604) 251-9718 · fax (604) 251-9738